Rude Boy Cop

Rude Boy Cop

Vassell Ramsay

Disclaimer

The characters, events and places depicted in this book are fictitious. While some names of people, places or events might to be factual they are in fact fictitious. Any similarities to real person, living or dead are coincidental and not intended by the author.

ISBN: 978-0-9783505-1-2

Dedication:

This book is dedicated to the memory of my late parents, Thelma & Allan Ramsay, late brother, my sisters, my wife and our son.

I wish to thank those whose encouragement has culminated in the completion of this work. Special thanks to my wife, Pauline, our son, Bruce and my sister, Sharon for their continued support. I could never have done this without your unwavering support.

Chapter 1

Rolling out of the bed, James stood naked in front of the large window and watched as the leaves sway under the weight of lingering dew. He didn't even know what time it; he knew he had one hell of a headache from all the partying the night before.

Reaching for his watch, he saw her lying there on the bed, he'd almost forgotten about Sarah. She was on her side with the blankets pulled up to her neck. She smiled and looked peaceful.

Sarah was almost six feet tall and big boned. From afar, her kinky hair appeared like a mop against her brown skin. Watching her as she rolled over and pulled down the covers from her neck, he smiled as memory of their first meeting came back to him.

He met her 5 months ago while at a party thrown by an acquaintance, Jerry Floyd, in Newtown. As he entered the room and greeted Jerry, she walked up him. She was a black woman, with soft features and a dimple on her right cheek. Not wasting any time in making her intentions known; she found him attractive and wanted him. She always spoke her mind and she didn't care who heard it or even if you were with someone else.

Looking up at him, and extending her hand, she said, "Well hello there, you are a fine brother, do you want to have some fun tonight?"

"We have never met before but you sure do look fine tonight and what have I done for such an honor?" James replied as he took her hand; her fingers were long, soft and well manicured.

"I am Sarah Brown and you look like the man who could make me forget anything, even my own name. Am I right?" she laughed while flashing her beautiful smile.

He figured when a good-looking sister present such a challenge, it's difficult for him not to accept it.

"I am not sure what I could offer you but I am curious as to what you have to offer me? I am James Williams and may I get you a drink?" he replied.

"Aha, don't tell me, you are James, Williams, the rude boy cop I have heard about. Do you know how many guys run for cover whenever they hear your name? Never thought I would be so fortunate or unfortunate to meet you, this is going to be interesting after all. Yes I will have a rum and coke for sure."

"What could be so unfortunate for you to meet me, am I bad a person or you are the bad one?" he asked as he walked away.

Waiting for the drinks, her words lingered on his mind; she knew guys who were afraid of him. He also figured she might be a good contact to have.

James Williams, a hard-nose forty-seven year old cop, had spent almost twenty-five years on the force. He was a tall man, six feet and five inches, broad shoulders, dark brown eyes and a close crop of nappy hair on his head. Others see him as being ruggedly handsome but he would disagree with such an opinion. He grew up on the rough side of town and as such, he had to fight his way out.

With an absentee father, his mother while holding down two part-time jobs tried her best to bring him up the right way. As a rebellious child, he tested her. He found listening to his friends more important than what she had to say to him. Education at time was not high on his agenda; hanging out with other young boys, was.

Once he became involved in a fist-fight with an older boy and when it ended, the other boy left unconscious. Taken into custody but being a juvenile, he was sent to a juvenile center for a few months, and then returned to his mother.

Failing to change his ways, she shipped him off to her brother. His uncle made sure to curb his violent tendency and eventually got him on the straight and narrow path.

James slowly changed his outlook on life. No longer surrounded by his former friends, his needs changed.

At eighteen years old, his juvenile history sealed, he took the opportunity to keep it that way but never lost the rude boy mentality. He wasn't prepared to sit back and let anyone dictate his life; he remained head-strong, however, he learnt how to manage it.

By his early twenties, he decided to attend the Police College. It helped to control his anger. And now married with children, told his wife, Bev he would be going undercover to catch a criminal but there he was, being seduced by a beautiful black woman.

Returning with the two drinks, he handed one to Sarah and she gently caressed his fingers and smiled.

"Yes indeed, this will be a different evening for me and I had not even yet made my usual rounds," he thought.

"To answer your last question, I hope it's not unfortunate but if it were, maybe you could arrest me and have your way with me," she replied as she whispered in his ears.

Holding her hands, he walked to the dance-floor. For the next hour, they danced. They were each pushing the other to a sexual peak. As he reached for her ample butt, she simply danced around him while flashing her brilliant smile.

She enjoyed knowing others were watching her; it made her feel sexy. When the DJ slowed the music, they danced real close and James felt the heat from both their bodies flowing to his head. The look in her eyes told him, she wanted him.

Whispering in her ears, he said, "Would you like to get out of here for a while? It's getting real hot in here."

Flashing her hair, she said, "I thought you would never ask, yes I would love, let's go. Where do you want to go, maybe your place? We can't go to mine baby but don't worry; I don't have a man at home, my kids are there and I have to protect them."

"No need to explain to me, I understand. We can get a room down on the strip," he replied.

"Fine with me honey, hey, it's ok if we can't go to your place either, I understand, your old lady is home."

"How would you know I have a woman?"

"Now come on Johnny, may I call you so? Take a good look at yourself, you are an attractive black man and dressed to the nines. Somewhere, some woman must have a hold on you. I can't see you not having a wife or few ladies at your beck and call."

"Johnny is fine with me, let's go."

Later as they both lie spent in each other's arms, he told her about Beverly. She was his wife of sixteen years and the mother of their three children.

"Do you love her?"

"I'm fond of her and don't wish to have anything affect our marriage."

"It's ok, I like you but I don't want to wreck your home. I am old enough to keep a secret however I would like to continue to see you as you make me feel good in all the right places."

In the back of his mind, he kept saying, "No, we can't see each other," however the urges were strong and fresh in his mind.

Facing her, he saw the same smile that caught his eyes a few hours before. As she pulled him closer and kissed him, Bev was a fond memory. He was smitten by her beauty and sexual prowess. It was a night he would not easily forget.

Five months in, they were meeting often. Last night was no different; they met for dinner at an out-of-the way diner and followed it with a stop at the Delmar Motel. While he enjoyed her company, he didn't love her and didn't wish to have such a distraction at this time.

He had too many things on the go; most of all, he was forsaking his wife and children back home and still on the trail of Lucas Wise otherwise called Snake.

```
` ` `
```

Snake was one of a group of well-known local criminals who often openly flaunt their activities. Many times, the Police would arrest their foot-soldiers but never be able to snag the top brass.

They were hiding behind thick walls and nobody willing to sell them out; no matter what the price. Snake was considered to be one of those guys but the Police could never pinpoint his whereabouts. They knew he was malicious and impulsive. Early in his life, he lost his father and had to fend for himself.

As a young man, he beat another man almost to death and so he began a criminal path which led him to human trafficking and drug smuggling. He was a tall and heavy-set man with a partially bald head upon his broad shoulders. He had a pudgy face with ice-cold blue eyes and he was known to have frequent plastic surgery and change his features.

Being a smooth operator, he had his men flashing money around especially to the homeless. He considered himself to be a lady's man and as such surrounds himself with beautiful ladies. But make no mistake; he was ruthless if crossed. When one of his women failed to turn in her money after a night's activity, he had his men beat her as a warning to the other women. The information on the street said he was involved in trafficking under-age girls and gun running.

Once he began to turn young girls into prostitutes, James drew the line. If for no other reason than the fact he, himself, had a daughter. He had been investigating Snake for the past four months and each time he got close, he slipped through his fingers.

```
```

As the sun rose across the horizon, James knew it was time to report to the station. He couldn't keep telling Bev he was working all night. Tapping Sarah on her shoulder, he watched as she stretched out her long arms and opened her big brown eyes.

The covers slowly slipped down her body exposing one breast, then the other, and he smiled. By the time she had completely stretched out her arms, she lay completely naked from the waist up before him and said, "Come and get some."

Knowing they had to leave shortly, he said, "It's time to get going, I want to head down to the station before I go home."

"Sure you don't want some more of this?" she asked as she gently stroked her breasts.

"You know I would love to have some more but right now, we both have things to get done."

"Alright, don't say I didn't offer it to you, I will be ready in a couple of minutes but you go ahead. Will I see you next week as usual?"

"We will see how it works out. Why don't you give me a call down at the station? I have to get going, catch you later," he said as he kissed her and walked out the door.

```
```

James got to his precinct as the night shift was leaving. On his desk, were two messages; one from Bev and the other from Rick, his street contact. Calling Bev, he thought the worst as he dialed the number.

"Hi honey, I heard you called. What's up?"

"Hi dear, when you are coming home please bring some bread and a jug of milk."

"Sure thing honey, where are the kids, are they up yet? I want to take you all shopping later."

"Oh, any special reason?" she asked.

"Nah, I guess I haven't spent much time with you guys and I need to do it sometimes. I will see you in a little while," he said as he took a deep breath and leaned back in his chair.

Remembering Rick; he decided to call him; he was one of his contacts. Rick, a street-level hood, thought he was too smart to be caught, until he turned up on James' shift. He was a lanky, freckle-faced, red haired kid. He was twenty-eight years old and while his birth certificate confirmed this, he looked no older than nineteen. He tells everyone James arresting him was a blessing.

When James first arrested him, he saw something in him and made him try and help him to get a place of his own. In turn he promised to give him the scoop on the low lifers. They formed a strange friendship which produced some good leads.

"Hello, is Rick there? Let me speak with him, thanks."

After a few minutes Rick came on the line.

"Hi Rick, Jim here, what's new buddy?" he asked.

"Yeah, what can I do for you?" he replied while looking at his friends.

"I know you can't talk freely now so why don't you meet me in a few minutes at the corner at Don's coffee shop. I want to check on something," said James.

"Alright man, cool; I will see you when next you are in town," he replied while still watching his roommates; he knew they were wondering.

"It's ok guys, 's a hustler I met on the streets a few days ago and he gave me a few dollars, not to worry, no one is coming around here," Rick said to his roommates as they relaxed.

James grabbed his jacket and threw it over his shoulder and strolled out the door.

"Hell, I forget Bev wanted me to get some bread and milk, she is going to be mad," he said.

Approaching the intersection, he saw see Rick standing with his foot resting against the wall, puffing away on his cigarette. James pulled up beside him and he jumped in the car without it even stopping.

"Hey Det. Williams, sorry I had to talk to you like that back there, I had company."

"No problem, what do you have on Snake?"

"I heard a stripper down at the Elves Club might be a good contact. Her name is Chili, I have never spoken with her but the word on the street is she has a few girls working for her at the club. The story is she does a few lines now and again with some real hardcore dudes so she might be a link to check out?"

"Ok Rick, listen, here are a few dollars, stay low and let me see about this Chili, maybe she can provide the lead I am seeking."

"Take care for now Det. Williams and you know if I hear anything at all, I will let you know; you can count on me."

Slowing the car down, he watched as Rick skipped out of the car before the lights changed. Soon he blended in the crowd with all the morning shoppers.

` ` `

Stopping by the corner store, James saw two young men mulling around the check-out counter with hands in their pockets. He found it strange, while both men stood at the counter; they did not have anything in their hands or on the counter. The sales clerk appeared to be on edge. Passing them, he stopped by the fridge, selected a bag of milk then a loaf of bread. Standing before the pop machine, he selected his favorite soda while continuing to watch the men.

The falling soda caused both men jump and they stared at him.

Standing next to both men, he waited for a minute before saying, "Are you boys buying something or you're going to stand there and stare?"

"Old man, if you know what's good for you, you would get the hell out of here," said the smaller of the two

Turning to face them, and frowning, he replied, "Now why would I want to do? Tell you what; I am going to give you a minute to change your minds from whatever you had planned. Today definitely will not be your best day so do us all a favor and walk away."

Looking up at James, the bigger of the two reached inside of his waist; he never got the chance. In a split second, he found himself on the ground, holding onto his scrotum and writhing in pain.

His partner stood there in shock, watched as his friend screamed. Looking up, he saw James' badge and gun. Resigned, he placed his hands above his head and knelt on the floor.

With shaking hands, the sales clerk raised his head over counter, when he heard James identifying himself.

A squad car soon arrived and the men were taken away.

"Thank you officer, your goods are on me."

Exiting the store, he replied, "No need to, I was just doing my job and happened to be at the right place and the right time."

Chapter 2

Driving up his driveway James saw Bev through the kitchen window. Bev
was a few years younger than his forty-seven years and she looked good.
She kept herself in shape by going to the gym as often as she could and still
cared for their children while maintaining a part-time job.

Unlike James, she grew up in a more well-to-do home environment
with both parents at home and actively involved with her and her sister's
upbringing. She was no push-over; she always stood up for what she
believed to be right at all cost. When she first met him, she was attracted to
his ruggedness and his take-no-prisoner attitude, someone who took
charge. Her golden brown complexion and curves in the right places made
her a complete package.

They were married within a year of their first meeting and he believed
neither she nor he ever regretted the decision. She understood the nature
of his job and never asked too many questions. For the first few years she
always worried about him while he worked on the drug squad. As time
went by, she accepted certain risks came with the job.

Whenever he came home and talked about the job or some punk they
arrested, she rolled her eyes without making a comment. With the grocery

bags in hand, he stepped out of their old clunker of a car and walked through their front door.

He felt nice to be home; even though he had a good time with Sarah, he needed to be with Bev and the children. Dropping the bags on the kitchen table, he held her real close. She felt warm and snuggled deeper in his arms.

"I need you."

"Go have a shower first, you still smell of the streets, you take your work home with you," she said with a sly smile.

He quickly walked towards the shower and showered. He was in and out of the shower in a flash and wrapping the towel around his waist, walked into the bedroom but Bev wasn't there.

"Hey honey, come in here for a minute, will you."

The pita-pata of little feet heading his way, made him dash for a housecoat. John and Sharon burst though the bedroom door and into his arms; he had not seen them in 24 hours. Dudley, the oldest at thirteen years, saw himself as a young man and young men don't run into their father's arms.

John and Sharon were nine and eleven respectively and still saw him as daddy. Holding them both, he embraced them as Bev walked through the door with a resigned look on her face as if to say, "Better timing next time."

"How are my youngsters doing this morning?" he asked as he kissed each of them.

Both kids began to speak at the same time. "Daddy, we are happy you are home, mom says you are going to take us shopping."

"Ah yes, I see mom told you guys about our planned trip. Now I know why you both ambushed me this morning. Yes we will be going shopping later today. Where would you guys like to go? "

"The Zone playhouse," said John.

"No, I want to go the mall," responded Sharon.

"Ok, ok, let's ask mom where we should go seeing you both want to go separate places. What about Dudley; isn't he interested in going with us?"

Bev said, "You know Dudley, he is in his own world; he and his music. He plans to go out with his friends from next door and we don't have to worry about him for now. Now let's see, oh, we should go the mall for a change."

"What do you guys say, we all agree about the mall?" James asked as both children sitting on their bed, anxiously awaiting the adults' decision.

"Yeah," they said. Finally they both agreed on something and James wondered if the kids' play area was the deciding factor.

` ` `

The mall had always been one busy place, any time of the day. After driving around for 15 minutes, he finally found a spot only to have a young man slip in ahead of him. Pulling up behind him, he called out to him, "Hey you, I have been waiting for spot and you took it, what gives?"

"Screw you, buddy," he said, giving James the finger.

"That's it; no one and I mean no one does that to me," said James as he jumped out of the car with his badge and gun in hand, "You pipsqueak, you want to give me the finger again?" he said while standing near the car door.

Seeing the badge and gun, the man turned pale and pleaded with him while trying to restart his car, "I'm sorry officer, you can have the spot, I didn't realize you were a cop."

"It shouldn't matter if I'm a cop or a private citizen, wait your turn and not butt in before others," he replied.

James felt good watching him skirting around the parking lot in search of another spot, "Serve you right, you dickhead," he murmured under his breath as he got back into his car.

Bev seething under her breath glared at him. The kids looked scared and speechless.

"It is ok kids; you don't think I would have shot him, did you? You know daddy would never do it, the man was rude and I had to let him know I didn't care for his behavior. What say we go and get some ice-cream?"

The thought of ice cream jolted them back to their old selves, all except Bev. Once they were out of the car and away from the kids, she spoke her mind.

"You know you didn't have to pull your gun on the guy back there. Showing him your badge would have been enough; you have got to stop using force when people get under your skin."

"Listen baby, I am a cop, I have done this for way too long and am not going change right now. You of all people know how much I hate assholes and baby, he was a big one," he smiled as he pulled her close to him.

"I want you to be careful, someday someone is going to try and make you pay."

"I know you worry about me but it is cool, believe me, I won't take too many unnecessary chances, I want to be around you and the kids for a long time to come."

Sharon and John were waiting for them by the ice cream counter. Soon they were all slurping on their cones trying to eat as fast as they could.

"Come on dad, I want to go in this store, they have some great toys in there. Mom, can I go inside while you guys finish your cones?" John asked.

"Sure dear, you may go inside but don't touch anything, you hear?"

` ` `

Soon they all finished eating and entered the store to join John who by now was playing with a gadget. James knew it his favorite toy as anytime he saw it on the TV; he wouldn't walk away until the ad finished. Next it was Sharon's time, and Bev knew exactly what she wanted. She had not any interest in toys; she wanted her ears to be pierced and soon, she was sitting in a chair at Accessories and Things. She never winced a bit as the attendant made the holes in her ears. She was rewarded with a pair of small diamond stud; the smile on her face was worth the cost of the earring.

Thinking of getting something for Bev, he knew the place to get it. As he steered the group toward Silk Shoppe, she held him back.

She said, "Oh no, we aren't going in there, not today with the kids. Let's go over to Pearle's and look around."

At first, he was disappointed however he understood what she was saying. Walking into Pearle's, she picked out a short and sexy spaghetti strap dress. His wide smile was a sign he approved.

It was time for him to return home to get some rest before he left for his evening shift. He still hoped to have some quiet time with Bev before he went to work.

Stepping out in the blazing sun, the heat reflected off the vehicles and momentarily blinded James as they walked to the car.

` ` `

Back home, the kids rushed from the car, calling for Dudley, as they wanted to tease him for not coming with them.

Looking at James, she asked, "Do you think we will have enough time, you know, with the kids roaming about?"

"I am sure we will, I am going to lock the door," he said as he got up and locked it.

As he turned around, she slowly stripping away her clothes, as each piece fell, he got more excited.

Half an hour later, he collapsed in her arms feeling spent and listening to her heart beating against his chest.

"That was some workout," she said, rolling onto her side next to him.

"Yes, you make me feel complete."

"Maybe you will change your shift now you remember how good it is," she jokingly said while nudging him with her elbow.

"Now honey, you know what it would mean? I would have to change my platoon and maybe end up with a desk job and you know how much I hate. I have worked hard to be where I am now and would hate to lose it all. Tell you what? Suppose I come home during my shift, would that help?"

"No you won't, I don't want you coming home in the middle of the night and leave me here all by myself. You complete your shift and come home; we will work it out. Jimmy, are you listening to me? Well I'll be damn, you fell asleep on me, and I must have worked you out."
"Heh, wake up, it's time for dinner."

The loud voice echoed in his ears and he woke up startled.

For a few moments, he did not know where he was. Getting up, he headed for the shower. The water felt warm and inviting against his naked skin, the only thing, the only person, missing was Bev.

The sweet smell of curried chicken filtered upstairs and he felt hungry. He slipped into a pair of gray casual slacks and a dark green turtleneck before exiting the bedroom.

"Hi Dudley, I didn't see you this morning. Did you have a good time with your friends?" he asked.

"Hi dad, sorry I never saw you when you came home. Yeah, I had a good time today with Paul and Errol."

"Yeah?" enquired James.

"I meant yes dad, sorry."

He and Bev chatted for a while and she noted, "I'm not pressuring you but the kids are growing up fast. You need to spend some time with them."

"I understand what you are saying, I will to try and make some changes if possible."

Looking at his watch, he realized he was going to be late once more to get to the station and got up to leave but she though he was trying to get out of the conversation

"We will talk again when you get home and you can't run away," she said.

He was 45 minutes late for the beginning of his shift and had even missed roll call.

"Williams, you are late again. What the hell am I going to do with you, can you tell me? Come into my office."

"What are you all looking at?" he said as he slammed the door behind James.

"Jim, how is it going? You know I can't let those rookies see you coming in late and not say anything, they would eat me alive out there," he said with a smile.

"I know Paul, how are you and the family? It's been a while you have been over to our house, we have to change that soon."

"Yes we will have to work on it. Tell me, how is the case on this guy, Snake, any new development? Maybe we should put someone else with you."

"Paul you know I prefer to work alone. I do have a lead and I'm going visit the Elves bar tonight to find a dancer name Chili; I hear she might be running with the crowd."

"Ok, as long as it's moving along, we don't need any extra hands but be careful, I don't want to have to tell Bev something happened to you. Her sister would probably kill me if something happened to you."

Staff Sergeant Harris was married to Bev's sister and she had him where it hurts; when she said jump, he would only asked how high, never why.

On a one on one basis however, James shared a good relationship with Sgt. Harris; as brothers-in-law, they surprisingly enjoyed each other's company away from work and always looked out for each other.

Paul had been on the Police force for a long time but unlike James, he became tired of working on the streets and took the first opportunity away from it. One thing remained constant between them both; the love of the job but in varying degrees.

As James had to go out on the road, Sergeant Harris opened his door and bellowed, "Get the hell out of my office and don't show up here late tomorrow."

"Right Sgt. I hear you," James said with a sheepish grin as he slowly closed the door behind him.

Now in his unmarked car, he drove to the Elves bar down on Rich Street; Chili now in his sight as he needed some answers.

Chapter 3

In the Summer evening, the street were busy with women strolling about in short dresses and guys with their shirts open to expose their chests, blowing kisses at the ladies. Some were seen hustling on their way home with their shopping bags over their shoulders, trying their best to maneuver around those hanging around.

The Elves bar stood out like a sore thumb at the foot of Rich Street. The pink neon lights shun brightly and girls scantily dressed, standing in its entrance. James slowed down as he came abreast of the front doors and took a quick glance inside. It was dark with flashing strobes of light and loud noise escaping outside.

Parking a few streets past the bar, he watched the action before strapping on his .22 to his ankle.

Standing amongst the crowd, he waited in line and paid his $15.00 entrance fee. After a brisk search, he entered and picked a table in the back of the room. Ordering a rye and ginger, he sat back and observed the room, several ladies dancing on the stage.

Chuckling, he noted several women were also in the audience and they were not dancers.

As the music changed, all the ladies scampered off the stage, now it was time for the star attraction. Chili, an extremely attractive young woman, had a voluptuous body with curves in all the right places.

Seeing her, James understood why she was the star attraction. Most men would dream of making it with her and she played on it through her suggestive dancing.

She was a smart woman; she made all the right moves and teased them so much they were soon throwing their money onto the stage. The more she showed, the more money they tuck in her g-string or placed in front of her. Eventually her act came to an end and another dancer took her place. As she exited the stage to a room full of horny guys, they all howled for an encore.

For the next several minutes, James watched her making her rounds. Other dancers appeared at his table but he had no interest in them. He was there for one person; Chili, and no one else. Twenty minutes later, she arrived in his corner, "Hello Chili, do you care to share a drink with me?"

"Why, certainly, thank you," she said, taking the seat in front of him.

"You sure put on an exciting show earlier with all the guys and the ladies too going crazy for you."

"Yes, it is always fun to watch you guys get all excited, it makes my job a lot more fun and easier. The ladies surprised me though, never thought they would enjoy it as much. So what are you doing here tonight? You look out of place here."

"Well, I am told you might be able to tell me where to find Lucas, you know, Snake."

Tightening her jaws, she swallowed hard and but said nothing.

"You do know him, right?" he asked.

Leaning back in her chair, she said, "I am not sure if I understand what you are asking me, why you think I know him and if I do, so what? Are you a cop or something?"

"Look, no, I am not a cop; I want to get a score from him. Why do you think I am a cop? A friend told me he could help me move some stuff, you know."

"So how come you know him as Snake? Only a few people ever call him such. Lucas doesn't like to have anyone looking for him, tell you what? What you say your name is?"

"Jimmy," he replied.

"Alright Jimmy, I have to go back on stage in a few minutes, why don't you meet me by my room after my next show and maybe we will talk. Don't worry; you will know my room when you get there. Nice talking with you."

As she walked away, it all seemed way too easy for him.

Experiences told him most dancers were protective of their friends and were never quick to give information about them. He could not place his fingers on it but something told him to keep an eye out for the unexpected. He didn't trust too many people right now. Looking around, he saw her chatting with a couple bouncers and never thought much about it.

Her second show lasted for almost 20 minutes and while the crowd wanted more, she bid them goodbye without an encore.

Waiting for 10 minutes, James walked towards her room as she instructed.

Strolling along the long and dark passage, he saw her pictures along with the other dancers, hanging along the walls. Finally standing in front of her room; it had a star on the door and he gently knocked on it before turning the handle and stepping inside.

With a foot inside the door, he felt a crushing blow to the right side of his face. Falling outside the door, his eyes briefly out of focus, it looked like three people were standing at the entrance. Shaking his head; he saw only two standing over him.

He didn't know which one had punched him and wasn't about to ask. They both hauled him like a rag-doll through the door and plopped him down on a chair.

Their faces inches away from his, shouting, "What the hell do you want with Lucas? Who told you about Chili, who the hell are you?"

Before he answered, another blow came across his face and he shook his head, he tried to size up the situation. Neither one bothered to search him; they didn't know how to do their job.

Playing along, he wanted to see how much they would tell before it became dangerous. He couldn't afford to be hit once more; the punches were beginning to take its toll on his head.

"I am Jimmy and Big Al told me I could get some stuff from Snake, all guys," he said.

"And he told you about Chili?" asked the big man.

"Now how the hell would I otherwise know to ask for her? He said she would be able to pass on my information to him. Come on guys, give me a break."

"Are you a cop or what? No one comes here and asks for Lucas without a real reason and furthermore, we never heard of you. What exactly is it you want to move, let's see exactly who you are," said the big man, walking towards James.

Jumping up, James kicked him in the shin. His training told him, everyone had a weak spot and he watches as the man doubled over. Before his partner realized it, he had a chair across his face and in a flash, he was laid out cold.

Looking over the place, James knew there was no point in sticking around; soon others would come searching for their friends. Hurrying to the door, he cautiously opened it. Staring back, he saw Chili hiding behind a desk, eyes wide open. Walking towards her, he changed his mind; there would be another time.

Outside, the cool evening breeze felt good on his sore jaw. He had to give it to the bouncers though, they had a good punch but he had been there before and always survived. He rushed to his car and sat there while considering his next move.

The night was still young and he didn't care to call it a night. The ladies of the night were still hanging out on the streets. He thought they could shed some light on his elusive fugitive so he slowly pulled away from the alley and drove down the road.

The first woman to see him was eager to chat, looking for a good time or at least, some quick money.

"Hey honey, how about a ride for awhile?" she asked.

He chuckled at her approach and thought. "I have not heard such before. Guess they have been arrested for soliciting so many times, they needed a new approach."

"Get in the car," he said as he pushed open the door.

Slipping in the front seat, she quickly wanted to exit; she had seen the Police radio.

"Relax, I am not here to bust you or harm you, I need some information. Maybe you can help me, I'm Det. James Williams."

"I am Devine and I have heard of you. Many of the girls and their boyfriends are afraid of you."

"You mean the girls and their pimps, right? You have no reason to fear me; it's the pimps I am after."

"I can't speak for others but what you see is what I am all about."

Devine was once a pretty young woman but her choice of work had taken a toll on her. Said she was 30, but like 50 with dark rings around her eyes.

"So Devine, can we talk?"

"Sure, I'm here and you have the power to do whatever. What do you want to talk about anyway?"

"Have you ever been by the Elves bar? Have you ever seen the dancer Chili?"

Relaxing a little, she said, "We all know that bar, sometimes we go there with a date if he wants. I have seen Chili in there but have never spoken with her; 2 or 3 guys always surround her. She and another woman are often times seen hanging onto the arms of one particular guy."

"How much do you know about her and what can you tell me about the other woman and the guy?"

"Ah, the other one is about five feet, nine inches, a well built black woman and the guy is tall and partially bald with slick black hair on the sides. He is always dressed in real fancy suites, looks like he could be the owner or he has some connection to it.

"Ok, is there anything else you can tell me?"

"Well, he doesn't like anyone to look directly at him. Is this person you are interested in or Chili and the other woman?"

He knew she was describing Snake but didn't wish to share any information with her, never knowing the connections on the streets.

"Not, I am only interested in Chili and the other woman?"

"All I hear from the other girls is, when they share a few lines in the bar, it's usually done downstairs in a special room. Oh, I think the other woman is called Sarah but I am not certain."

Shifting in the seat, she continued, "I could try and find out more for you but right now I should be getting back, my boyfriend will be looking for me soon and this talk won't get me any money."

"Yes I guess I have taken up too much of your time. Here are a hundred dollars and thanks for your time. Can I call on you again?"

"Yes, Det. you can call again, providing you make it worth my time," she chuckled.

"As long as you understand this conversation never occurred, I won't give you a hard time."

"Det. Williams, you are not such a bad person as I have heard. Still, I wouldn't want to be on your wrong side, I think you could be a real bad dude."

Tucking the money in her purse and with a last look at herself in the mirror, Devine dashed out of the car in a hurry.

James sat for a few minutes before gunning the sedan down the road beneath the neon lights. He now knew something he didn't when he first walked into the Elves bar; Sarah may be a part of the group and Snake might also be the owner or at least, he has some interest in it. He would play along with Sarah to see what she had to offer and also check on the ownership.

`` `

Late at night, the ringing telephone startled Snake. Picking it, he saw the call came from Chili.

Getting out of bed and away from his woman, he quietly walked to the bathroom and closed the door behind him.

"Hi Chili, what's up? Sorry I didn't come to see you tonight; I will make it up to you."

"Yes, Lucas, everything is ok, I'm calling to tell you a guy came here earlier tonight asking for you. He said Big Al told him you could help him get some stuff. He also put a beating on Ed and Tom. I have never seen him before but he called you Snake."

"What does this guy look like?"

"Well, he is tall like you and he sure looked like a cop."

"Ok, thanks for letting me know, I will have to check him out. Don't say anything to anyone; tell the guys I will make it up to them."

"They are in the hospital right now."

Running his hand through his hair, he said, "Shit, this guy is a mad man. Ok, I'll deal with it. I'll see you later babe."

"What was that all about?" the woman lying next to him, asked.

"Nothing, Sarah, something down at one of the bars, go back to sleep, we will talk about it later."

Pulling the covers over his head, he couldn't sleep; the information bothered him.

Chapter 4

Friday night, and the local thugs were having a ball. Calls were coming across the Police radio of various disturbances across the city; one particular report intrigued James. Two bouncers were found beaten in the back of Elves bar and no-one saw it happen.

It was 1.30AM and James felt like calling it a night, not much more could be done. The thought of waking up next to Bev for a change rather than coming home after the sun came up, excited him.

Arriving home at 2 am, he showered and snuggled next to Bev. She held him tight and both were soon snoring. Saturday morning and he woke up to the smell of freshly brewed coffee. Rolling over, he found the bed empty. Bev was an early riser and was up making breakfast.

Luckily for him, this was his weekend off and he had chores around the house. Dragging himself to the bathroom, he had a shave and shower, felt refreshed and was ready for a hearty meal.

` ` `

In the wee hours of the night, he kept thinking about Sarah and her possible connection with Snake. He needed to meet with her before their planned get together to find out what she knew.

Sunday morning took a long time to come for James; he needed to get things straightened out. Taking a stroll after breakfast, he called Sarah.

"Hi, I know we agree not to call each other at home, I'm hoping I could see you later tonight."

"Is everything ok Johnny? Yes I would love to see you if I can get away."

"Yes, all is well. Can't it be I want to see you?" he chuckled while saying these words.

"Ok, I will give you a call or a text later if I am able to see you."

"I look forward in seeing you," James replied.

Sitting in her living room, Sarah was perplexed yet excited; James broke his own rule of not contacting each other at home. She happy knowing he still had interest in her enough to break his own rule.

Walking towards her bedroom, she began to run her hands over her body as if to reclaim the sensation she felt when she with him.

"Mom, are you ok?" ask her daughter, Sharon.

Grabbing her gown, she tried her best to cover herself; she had forgotten her older daughter was home. Sheepishly she said, "Just checking myself for any lumps."

Darting into the bedroom, she shut the door behind her; she knew she had to be more careful as her daughter or someone else could have also heard her conversation with James.

In the evening, James snuggling with Bev, said, "I am running out for a short time to check on a lead."

Rolling her eyes, with her hands on her hips, she walked to the kitchen and handed him a cup of coffee.

Staring at him, she said, "Why do you bother to come home? You live for your work and why do they have to call you on your days off, couldn't someone else deal with this today?"

"Listen baby, you know I have to take any lead I can get whenever it happens, I'm sorry. You know I have been chasing this guy for some time now and I can feel it, I am going to catch him real soon."

"Make sure he doesn't catch you first."

Laughing, he said, "Snake catching me."

Seeing Sarah on a Sunday evening could be a good thing as he was also considering ending their relationship. Once he got the information he needed; there was no need to be with her. Bev would always be first and foremost. He didn't need this added distraction but again he had no one to blame but himself.

Arms folded on the dining table, Bev blurted out, "Why so many Police officers don't have time for their family. Jimmy, you don't have any other things going on the side, do you?"

Swallowing hard, he asked, "What do you mean things on the side, like what? Do you mean if I'm fooling around on you?"

"No, not what I meant, you know, like Mark who has a job on the side. I would hate to think you would be involved with someone else while I am working my butt off to keep you happy."

"Well not to worry my love, you are enough for me and I hope you believe me. To answer your question, no, I don't have a "job" on the side," he replied.

"Ok, and if you ever have the thought of fooling around, remember the kids upstairs, they need you more than I do."

"Bev I sense something might be bothering you, are you ok?"

"Yes I am fine; I wish you would spend less time on your work especially on the weekends. I don't get to see you often enough and as for the children, they will be all grown up and you will have missed the experience."

Holding her hand, he said, "Listen dear, like I said before, I will speak to Paul and see if he can assign some-one with me, which might reduce my time away from you and the kids. As for "outside jobs", you are the only job I need."

"You make sure you remember Jimmy."

It was time to meet Sarah and as he held Bev in his arms and kissed her, he had mixed feeling about leaving. One way or another, their affair could not continue, not after conversation with Bev.

Pulling into the motel grounds, he saw Sarah's vehicle parked to the side. Striding past the front-desk, he stopped in front of the agreed room, and gently tapped on the door two times.

The door opened slowly and sitting on the bed in a baby-blue teddy was Sarah with two glasses of wine.

Taking the glass from her, he walked to the bathroom and closed the door behind him. Pouring most of the drink down the drain, he walked back to the bedroom to find her beneath the covers, beckoning him to join her. Stripping off his clothes, he got under the covers and pulled her close.

Twenty minutes later, they collapsed on the bed with him rolling over onto his side and Sarah, on her stomach, both out of breath.

"That was something. I never knew you wanted me so much. We have been good for each other. Don't you think so, Johnny?"

"Yes we do mesh with each other; maybe that's why I broke my own rule," he replied.

"So tell me, why did you want to meet me today?"

"Well, I wanted to see you and couldn't wait for Thursday. Also, I was talking to a friend and she told me about Elves bar downtown. Have you ever heard of it?"

"Yes, I know the place and I have been there a couple of times, why do you ask?" she said.

"Who do you usually go there with, your girlfriends?"

"Sometimes, I go with my girlfriends, yes, and sometimes by myself. I am curious as to why you are so interested. Do you want to go there with me sometimes?"

"No, I wondered about it and if you knew someone named Lucas?"

"Lucas? I do know a few guys name Lucas so I am not sure who specifically you are referring to".

"I think he is Lucas Wise and goes by the nick name Snake," he said.

Turning to face him, she her bit her bottom lip and asked, "What do you want with him? I do know who you are speaking about. Is this why you ask me to meet you sooner?"

"Not at all, I wanted to see you but you also know I am a cop. I like to know about people who sometimes walk on the wrong side of the law."

"Do you think I might be involved in illegal activities along with this person down there?"

"I would hope not but again, I can't rule out anyone including you, sorry".

"Thanks a lot; I can't believe you would think that of me, especially after all this time we have spent together. I guess you were using me to get information but sorry, I can't help you".

"Sarah, you can't or you won't help? Listen, I am sorry, I need to know who this Lucas is. You know what? It was wrong for me to call you and ask you to meet me here. I will not bother you again; I will be on my way."

"Johnny, please don't go, I don't know anything."

He stepped out the door without even looking back. He knew she was the person Devine mentioned and she also knew Snake.

Bev smiled when he pulled into their driveway but she also wondered why he returned so soon. She was never the kind of wife who asked too many questions of him. She was happy to have him home and she quickly greeted him at the door with a hug.

"What's that smell, where you have been?" she asked.

Quick thinking, he said, "I picked a contact who happened to be a lady of the night and she sat in the car for a few minutes."

"Please go and shower and throw those clothes in the basket".

In the wee hours of the night, Sarah lying in the bed next to Lucas rolled over to face him, "I need to tell you something. I ran into a cop today. He wanted some information about you."

"Who is this person and exactly where did you meet him Sarah?"

"Oh, I met him at a party the other night and I think he is a cop. He said his name was Williams and no, I didn't give him any information. I told him if he wants to know about you he could meet me tomorrow."

"I wonder if he is the same person who went to the bar and asked about me. Ok, here is what you do, you and Bini set up the meeting and find out what you can about him. If he is a cop and he persists, you get him out of the way. In the meantime, I will have one of the guys check him out."

` ` `

Monday morning came and James switched roles with Bev; while she prepared for her day, he took the children to school. This day she would work for half a day and get back home in time to meet them.

Not she needed to work as he adequately supported the family; it gave her some freedom and self-worth. She enjoyed looking good and even liked when other men noticed her. She never encouraged them but nevertheless, she enjoyed the experience.

Chuckling, she recalled a time when at the gym and being approached by one of the trainers there who showed interest in her.

While she did find him quite attractive, she politely declined his offer to be more than acquaintances. Thankfully, he knew enough not to pursue it, and for she respected him even more. It however did make her feel special knowing he was much younger than her.

There were other men she found quite attractive and while tempted, she was a level-headed woman who prides herself on being in control.

Furthermore she knew James would never forgive her should she become involved with someone and he became aware. She also knew he would take it out on the poor soul who dared to get involved with her.

Getting ready for work, James telephone rang; it was from Sarah, "Would you like to meet at our usual place 6 PM today?"

Gritting his teeth, he paused for a second before responding, "There is nothing for us to talk about. It has all been said."

Pleading, her voice in a whisper, "I would love to see you today as I some information you might find helpful."

"Ok, Sarah, what kind of information do you have?"

"I know you ask me about Lucas, right?"

"Yes I am interested in finding him. I thought you didn't want to speak about him, Isn't it what you told me in no uncertain terms? Now you have a change of mind?"

"Johnny, I don't want to speak over the phone; I want to tell you in person. Please meet me and I will tell you what I know."

"All right, I will meet later, I have got to go."

Chapter 5

Driving away from the house, James saw Bev standing by the kitchen window, her words echoed in his mind. He couldn't to clear his head.

Along the tree-lined road, he noticed the open and bare land with several tumble weeds being pushed along by the wind. They rolled over and over as if they were trying to escape the wind. Some were lucky to find safety beneath an old house sitting in the middle of the open land.

The wailing sound of a siren caught his attention and he pulled aside. He realized he was in fact being pulled over. In his rear-view mirror he saw the young officer walking towards him.

Without looking in the car, the young officer said, "Your paper, please." James handed the documents to him and waited.

"Det. Williams, I am sorry to have bothered you, have a nice day," said the young officer as he finally looked at James through the car window.

"Not a problem, what's your name?"

"Constable Shane White, sir."

"Ah, what's your detachment and who is your supervising officer?"

"I am stationed at Detachment 35, and Staff Sergeant Fraser is the man, sir."

"Oh yes, Staff Sergeant Fraser, I know him quite well. Have you ever had any interest in working undercover young man?"

"Yes sir, but....."

"Listen, I like you and you are eager, I will speak with your commander and see what we can do. By the way, what was my infraction back there?"

"You went through the red light, sir."

"I didn't realize it, well thanks for being on the job, hopefully we will meet again, take care. Make sure to stop those reckless drivers and be safe out there."

Shane White was still new to the force, having recently graduated from the Police College. He was 25, six feet two inches tall and muscular with icy blue eyes and jet black hair. First of three children and still living at home with his parents, he was the apple of their eyes as the first to become a Police Officer.

As James sped away he realized he was late in meeting Sarah and she hated to be stood up. He felt angry at himself for worrying so much about being late for their meeting.

Pulling into the hotel parking lot, he saw her through the window, pacing the floor. Parking some distance from the entrance, he scanned of the area; he did not like surprises. He waited for a few moments before exiting the car and slipped through a side door.

Spotting him, she rushed into his arms and held him tight.

Pulling her away, he led her to a corner of the room and try as he might, he couldn't get a word in. She appeared to be in a hurry.

"Listen baby, I have the room ready for us, let's go upstairs."

"You have a room for us? You don't waste any time do you?"

"No I don't, I know you told me you didn't want to have anything to do with me anymore and I can't blame you. I have the information you need. So you see, this a win-win situation for both of us. You are not too upset with me are you?"

Inside the hotel room, she began to kiss him all over. His promise to Bev came back and hit him.

Holding her arms, he sat on the bed, pulling her down with him, "Sarah, I need you to understand something, we can't keep doing this. I agreed to meet you this evening because you said you have information on Snake. Bev is also asking questions about the frequent calls at various times of the day."

Jumping off the bed, with arms on her hips, she appeared disappointed. "Are you telling me, you only came because I said I have information about Lucas? I thought you cared enough about me to want to be with me. Frankly, I don't care what Bev has to say, maybe I should give her a call and let her know I am sharing you with her."

"You wouldn't dare call her. Do not even think about speaking with her, you hear me?" Moving away from her, he continued, "Listen, I do care about you, but you know my family and my job do come first. I told you unless you have real information about this man, there's nothing more for us to say or do."

"Ok, Johnny, I am sorry, I won't call her but I can't believe all I meant to you is having a good time and getting information about Lucas. Is that why you befriend me in the first place?"

"Look here Sarah, let's be honest, you were the one who came onto me, in case you forget, and you were looking for a good time."

"Well I'll be dammed, I have never been reminded before but it's good to know. Well mister "good-times," those days are over as of right now and the information about Lucas? You can forget about it, all this time being with you; I thought you cared about me. You can go find another easy lay."

Looking down at her, he turned and walked through the door. Strolling to his car, his stomach tightened, he felt a sense of guilt and relief all at once. He had all intention of ending their affair once there was some news about Snake.

"There would be other Sarah," he thought.

Slipping behind his steering wheel, he sat there for a few minutes thinking of his next move. He still needed some answers. He decided he would pass by Detachment 35 and speak with Sergeant Fraser.

After driving aimlessly around for a while, he believed Sarah knew a lot more than she had been letting on. He would follow her and see where she goes so he swung around and drove back towards the hotel.

It didn't take him long before he saw her car cruising down the street. Pulling over quickly, he watched her from a distance as she kept on driving while doing her make-up. She eventually turned a corner and he pulled out after her.

A kilometer down the avenue he saw her car parked by a store and she was chatting with a stocky looking male. They both kept looking behind them. James made a mental note of the store-front and kept on going; he would return.

Some distance away, he parked in a secluded area, exited the car and waited. From afar, he saw her gesturing and appeared to be in a heated argument.

Wanting to know what was happening, he decided to retreat to one of his old tricks. From deep in his old canvas bag, he pulled out one of his many disguises: that of an old man, and slipped into his alto ego: a homeless person.

Walking hunched over and with a cane, James lumbered up the road towards Sarah.

Along the way, young boys were shouting at him, "Hey old man, get off the sidewalk."

Without even looking at them, he continued his journey feeling proud of his disguise and getting closer to Sarah. Soon he was next to them and listened.

"How could you let him get away, I thought you said you had him wrapped around your little finger?" said the stranger.

"Listen Bini, I gave it my all; he is married and still has strong feelings for his wife."

"Well you need to do whatever you can to get back in his good books or Lucas will not forgive me. You don't want him to become upset with me because you know what would happen."

"I will try and contact him again but I am not sure if he would ever want to see me again. You should see how he looked at me and walked away, he had a cold stare like he was looking right through me."

"No Sarah, you will not try, you are going to contact this man and lead him to me. I don't care how you do it, get it done. In the meantime, we have a guy on the force; I will try and speak with him as soon as possible. Lucas needs some lose ends to be tied up."

James' ears perked up when he heard Snake had a contact within the Police Force. Now he understood why they were never able to catch him

Quickening his steps as he passed them by and ducked into the first store he came upon. Inside, he took a deep breath; now it was clear to him, she wasn't interested getting to know him, and she was working for Snake.

James also had a new problem; a Police man was on the take. Looking through the store window, he watched her pulling away, looking worried. Looking behind him, he saw the cashier looking at him in a strange manner and so he smiled and quickly purchased a chocolate bar.

``` ` ` ` ```

Walking back to the storefront where he saw her, he placed his face up to the window and looked in. There did not appear too much activity happening in there. There were no shelves or any goods in there.

A deep voice behind him caused him to jump, "What are you looking at old man? Walk away if you know what's good for you gramps."

Slowly turning around, he looked up into the face of hell. His arms and legs were massive and reminded James of the cartoon Popeye, his voice escaping from somewhere deep within his gut.

Stepping out his striking range, he said, "Sorry sir, I wanted to see what
```

they might be selling, I'll be on my way."

"You should be careful, next time you never know what might happen to you," he said and slammed the door shut.

Hastening away James kept looking behind; making certain no one was following him. Reaching his car, he quickly stripped off the disguise and pulled away: he had learnt enough for the evening.

He eventually called it a night, and headed out but, wasn't ready to go home, reaching for his phone, he called a friend.

"Hello Sue, up to having some company now?"

"Jay, why are you calling me so late? I guess I could do with some company, where are you now?"

"I am around the corner; I will be there in two minutes."

Walking through the door, he pulled her into his arms. They didn't waste any time as they both knew why he was there. Sue was another of his many women on the side and as much as he promised himself to get away from them all, he still much drawn to them. He would leave in the wee hours of the night.

James woke up in the late the next day to find Bev had left with the children to visit her parents. The house was deathly quiet: too much so for him. He decided to run the name of the store through the police system; "Greaves Shipping Inc."

Amongst the list of its owners were Sarah and two others, whose names didn't ring a bell. With this new information, he decided to take a ride back downtown; one of his contacts should be able to tell him more about the place.

He didn't get too far before he saw Anne. She was another lady of the night who had the fortune of running into him several years ago. She once had a boyfriend, Miki who was more of a pimp than anything else.

One night in a drug induced stupor, Miki thought she had not turned enough tricks or she was holding out on him. He wanted to let his knife do the talking. After cornering her in a dark alley, he began to carve her face.

Luckily for her, James was passing by when he heard her scream. Running from his car, he rushed to her aid only to be confronted by this madman.

"Drop your weapon; it doesn't have to go down like this."

With froth falling from his mouth, Miki turned and approached James, "This isn't your concern. This is between my woman and me."

"For the last time, drop the knife. I don't want to shoot you."

With the knife held high, Miki approached James who while calling for ck-up, fired two bullets into his chest.

Anne screams echoed in the dark alley, still clutching her face as blood flowed between her fingers. Collapsing near Miki, she wasn't sure if she should try and cradle her dead boyfriend or save herself.

Anne was soon on her way to the hospital while Miki headed to the morgue. The Police inquiry cleared James of any wrongdoing as there were several witnesses who vouched for him.

That was several years ago however, the memories made it feel like it was a short time ago. It was also something James could not forget. It was the first time he had taken another person's life. He had several sessions with a psychologist to get the images out of his mind, and now and again, he relives the ordeal.

Anne had not forgotten either; she knew Miki would have killed her, had then unknown policeman not intervened. She was forever grateful. It also helped that James visited her in the hospital and he never looked down at her or used his badge for illicit favors from her. They formed an alliance over the years.

Now years later, Anne was back on her feet, doing the same thing she did before but this time, she was going it alone. Every so often James would look her up to see how she was doing. It made her feel safe as she had an angel watching over her. Today would be no different than any other time except now he was trying to get information from her.

Anne spotted him long before he saw her; part of her instincts to observe her surroundings. With a big smile, she waved her hands wildly as his car came around the corner. He quickly pulled to the curb and she, continuing to smile, stepped into his car.

"How have you been James", she asked.

"Hi Anne, good to see you, I have been good"

"Come on now, you being good, the wife not allowing you out?"

"No, seriously, I am doing ok; it's nice to see you. When was the last time we saw each other?"

"Ok, I believe you, it has been quite awhile but it is nice to see you again. If it weren't for you, I would not be here, so thank you."

"No need to thank me, I happened to be at the right place at the right time. Any other officer would have done what I did and you have thanked me often enough."

"Oh I know, but still you were there and for I am eternally grateful to you. Now what brings you to my neck of the woods, so to speak?"

"Do you have a few minutes to talk with me?"

"Of course, what's up?'

"Do you know anything about a company called Greaves Shipping?" I am trying to find any information I can on this place."

"I have heard about it, but don't know much, I would be happy to see what I can learn. Do you want me to make some calls for you?"

"Find out what you can but please be careful, I don't need to have to come and rescue you once more," he said with a chuckle.

"I will be careful, but again, I would not mind if you were to rescue me once more. So how Bev and the kids doing, the kids are must be big now?"

"They are doing well and getting to be young men and young lady and yes Bev is doing well too. Oh by the way, have you ever heard of a Sarah Brown? "

"Sarah Brown? I am not sure if we are speaking of the same person but I do know a Sarah Brown who runs with a bunch of guys most people would not want to be associated with. Is she the person you are asking about?"

"Tell me what you know about this person."

"Well I know she hangs around with a guy I think his name is Lucas

Wise who operates a construction company, outside of town. Could it be the same person you are asking about?"

"I'm not sure if it's the same person we are speaking of."

He was happy for her and while he wished she would make a change in her type of employment, he respected her enough not to pressure her; dangerous as it, it's her life.

It's time for her to get back to her business, and while he offered to pay her for the time she spent with him, Anne would not have any of it, "You are my friend, I am happy just to help."

Chapter 6

James' mind now working over-time; chatting with Anne had confirmed some of the information he already heard. Now he knew of another business associated with the group and the location.

Travelling through the seedy part of town, he marveled at how a city like this could have two distinct neighborhoods; one affluent and the other run-down. He figured Snake must have chosen this location, out of sight and in an area where few people would ask questions.

He found the location but chose not to stop; the building did not look like much of a warehouse. Slowly driving by, he noticed an open side door and a few guys kept going in and out with wooden boxes. Not in any hurry to investigate, he planned to return later; he had lots of time on his hands.

The ringing telephone broke his thoughts and glancing at it he noticed it was Sarah. Frowning, he wasn't sure if he wanted to take the call but he was also curious as to why she tried to contact him.

Picking up the phone, he said, Hello."

"Hi babe, it's me, sorry for the way we parted, can I make it up to you?"

"What do you want?"

"Can we meet at the park off Brent Street, you know where, don't you? We can meet there in about thirty minutes if you want".

"I have a number of things to get done today, how about next Monday morning, around 11A.M?"

"I would like to see you as soon as possible; I need to apologize for my actions back at the hotel. Can't you try and see me today, even for a few minutes, please?"

"Why do you need to see me so urgently? I don't think we have anything to say to each other."

"I want to try and get back to where we were before all this went down. Johnny, I promise I will not take up too much of your time."

"Sarah, I have to think about this and get back to you but no, I won't be able to see you today".

Fuming under her breath, she tried not to blow her cool, "Alright, when would you like to meet and where if the park is not suitable for you?"

"Like I said, Monday will be a much better day for me and the park will be fine."

"Ok, I will see you then. I guess there is nothing I can do to change your mind?"

"No, not this time, sorry, I have got to go."

` ` `

At the station, he placed a call to Sgt. Fraser, an old acquaintance, "Hi Sgt. I ran into one of your young officers by the name White today."

"Ah yes, Const. White, he is a promising young officer; always looking for new challenges. What about him, did he do something out of the ordinary?"

"Not at all, he is focused on doing a good job and I told him I would speak with you on his behalf. In fact I am thinking maybe one of these days you would allow him to come over to my detachment and work with me on a project."

"Williams, I thought you enjoyed working alone? You never work with a partner so why the interest in my young officer?"

"Well, he impressed me and actually, I am becoming tired of running my one-man show. You know, we can't continue to do all this work forever, we have to get the young ones up to our standards so they will eventually take our place."

"True, listen, I will look into having him join you, let me know when and I will start the transfer papers. But you know you can't keep him forever."

"Sgt. I appreciate your assistance and promise I will take care of your officer and I owe you one."

"Alright, we will get it done for you, talk to you soon."

Late in the night, James called Bev, "Listen my love, I have to check a place out then I will be home."

She didn't appear to be too concerned, so she simply said, All right, see you when you get here

Gathering his bullet-proof vest and his guns, he strolled to his unmarked squad car: tonight, he would get some answers. He needed to find Snake and time was running out.

In the run-down neighborhood, he passed the warehouse in question and glanced around its surroundings. All appeared quiet with no noticeable movement in its general location. Finding an alley not too far from the building, he turned off the engine and waited for a few minutes. Putting on one of his many disguises, he checked both his guns and exited the car.

Hugging the wall, he moved towards the side doors. Once the sun disappeared, the place became a ghost town and this suited him. With a few quick steps, he found a door and slowly nudged it.

The door swung inwards and he waited a few seconds before entering: his ears keenly listening for any movement within. The wind whistle against his face as he slipped on his night vision goggles. Before him were several long wooden boxes lying on the floor. Snapping one open, he saw several high powered rifles and hand guns.

So engrossed in the find, he didn't hear footsteps running towards him. Once the lights came on, he was momentarily blinded. Ripping of the goggles, he jumped behind a rack of boxes and waited for his eyes to focus.

Bullets flew from two corners of the room and he returned fire and saw two persons fall to the ground. Once the two men were hit, the other man thought it was best to get out of there. Finding an open window, he jumped through it and kept on running.

Sitting in the corner, James calmed his nerves then checked on the wounded men; they were in no condition to escape. Groaning, both men held their wounded arm and leg.

"Who are you working for?" he asked.

Neither one had much to say except; "Can't you see we are bleeding? We need to see a doctor."

Pressing into the wound of the big man, James watched as he screamed in pain. As the pain overtaking his brain, he began to talk, "We know one person who runs this operation," he said.

"What is the name?" James asked while kneeling into the man's wound.

As the tears flow, the man shouted, "Sarah Brown is the person who runs this place. Now, we need to get to a doctor soon, please."

He called in the shooting and the cache of weapons found and the men were taken into custody and provided medical attention.

The danger of working alone finally dawned on him. He needed a partner as a back-up. The young officer White would be a good candidate.

Now it was time he went home and hugged Bev and check in on his children. He finally pulled into his drive-way and felt tired; he needed to unwind.

Turning off the car, he sat for a few minutes, retracing the events of the night and wondered out loud how Sarah was tied to Snake. How much did she know and how it would end. Bev rolled over in bed as he walked in and greeted him with a simple "Hi".

"Sorry for waking you up my dear."

"It is ok, I'm not sleeping, and I heard when you came in."

He had a quick shower and joined her in bed shortly after. Snuggling close to her, she felt good and he realized this was where he belonged. Dozing off, he dreamt Sarah and her cohorts were gunning for him. In cold sweat, he jumped up, frightening Bev.

"What's the matter?" she asked.

Patting her on the shoulder, he said, "It's a nightmare, nothing too serious my love, I will be fine. You try and get some sleep, sorry if I frightened you."

"I know something is bothering you, what it is?"

Sitting up, he said, "You know I have been investigating Snake and each time I uncover a little information, one woman's name keep coming up. I can't see her being the main person involved."

Bev listened and while she showed no sign of fright or fear for him, on the inside, her stomach tightened. She could only imagine the stress he was going through and with little hesitation, she said, "Maybe it's time you get yourself a partner."

He chuckled at those words, "I am thinking about it and I am looking into having another officer joining me."

Leaning on his shoulder, she said, "You should do it sooner rather than later."

"I promise I will look into it when next at the station,"

` ` `

Mid-day found James hard at work, behind his desk when he strolled into Sgt. Harris' office.

"Sgt. I think we have an informant amongst our officers. It's best we don't say anything but observe everyone for the time been."

Sgt. Harris said, "Unbelievable, one of our officers is a snitch? Ok, we will see if anyone starts acting strange."

As all the officers gathered in the briefing room, Sgt. Harris and James looked across the room but couldn't pint-point any particular officer.

"Today we are meeting a woman who has ties to Snake. We will not take any chances. Be diligent in our approach," Sgt. Harris announced.

Scanning the room, James noticed Const. White, "Welcome Const. White, glad to see you are joining us. Let's go everyone."

Looking around the room, James noticed one officer standing by himself looking intently on his cellular phone. He made no attempt to join them but kept looking at his cell phone and in the direction of the senior officers.

Walking over to him, James said, "Why aren't you leaving with the others? May I have a look at your cell phone?"

His face flushed a deep shade of red as he fumbled with the phone, "I... I was talking to my wife, sir."

Snatching it from him, James called out to Sgt. Harris over, "Look at this, he is sending a message about the operation. Who were you telling we are coming with full strength?"

"No one, I wasn't telling anyone about it."

"All right officer, you remain at the station, we will have a chat when we return. In the meantime, we are seizing this phone as evidence," Sgt. Harris said.

"Const. White, you will be my partner," said James

"Yes sir, what was that all about back there? I hope you don't mind my asking you?" Const. White asked

"When we return, I will fill you in, right now, let us focus on the task ahead," replied James

Shane felt intimidated being in the company of James. Words of his various arrests and convictions preceded him. Not many officers could walk in his shoes and here he was riding shot-gun with him. He had a big grin on his face yet he was aware of the seriousness of the situation.

"This isn't a rehearsal and we need to remain focus

Shane swallowed hard and said "Yes sir, I understand," while checking his rifle and side arms.

As they approached the park, James sped along the tree-lined avenue; he and his squad wanted to get there before Sarah. He was too late; at the park entrance; he glimpsed her car and she wasn't alone.

Alongside her vehicle was another car with two men standing outside with guns drawn. Radioing his squad, he said, "I'm going through and you cover the rear."

Lowering their heads, James and Shane drove right at the cars.

With guns blazing, Sarah's party jumped over their cars and continued firing as the car became airborne and crashed near a tree about twenty feet in front of them.

Running towards the destroyed car, the two men looked at each other, and grinned. Yanking open the driver's door, they saw it was empty. Turning to inform Sarah, they realized James and Shane were behind them.

Frozen for a few seconds, they tried to raise their guns at James and were gunned down.

Hanging his head down, Shane sat down on the grassy bank feeling sick; he had never fired his service weapon before much less having taken a life. His emotions were all over the place; not knowing if he should be happy or cry.

Standing by his side, James placed his hands on his shoulders, comforting him, "You did well and I am happy to have had you as my partner on this day. You never flinched; we both did the job we set out to do."

"I feel awful, this is a first for me."

"You will have some mixed emotions about this. Speak with our psychiatrist if you feel the need, I once did."

Shane looked at James puzzled, having never heard he too needed some counseling.

He however, felt proud to hear the officer he wanted to be like said he had done well. Standing up, he brushed off his uniform, shook James' hand and walked over to their crashed motor vehicle.

Sarah tried to run but she did not get too far as the remaining officers had secured the area. She could not believe her plan had failed; she had two of her most trusted men assigned to the job and they had not only failed but gotten themselves killed. She also knew Lucas would not be pleased.

Sitting in the back of the cruiser, she felt so out of place; there were steel bars around the windows and little she could do. She wasn't accustomed to such treatment as she had always lived the high life. She was read her rights with a chance to call her lawyer.

Looking towards the front seat, she heard the officers talking, Det. Williams strikes again, he never cease to amaze us with his tactical operation," one said.

She wished she had not seduced James the first time they met; but it was too late. She was heading for interrogation and possible much worse.

Chapter 7

Sitting on a cold steel chair and handcuffed to the table, Sarah opened one eye the next only to find the room pitch black. Her screams echoed in the empty room.

A switch flipped and the lights streamed across the table, momentarily blinding her. Blinking rapidly, she tried to shield her eyes from the brightness.

From the two-way mirror, James and his colleagues watched her, waiting for the right moment to enter the room. Soon, one officer, then another and finally James entered the room and stood before her.

Looking at the officers, she turned towards James and smiled.

Leaning across the table, he said, "You are being charged with murder as your action today has resulted in the death of two men. Do you understand the situation you are currently in, Sarah?"

Looking directly at him, she said, "If I give you the information you need, what will I be getting out of it?"

James asked, "What exactly do you have to offer us at this point?"

"Make me a deal and I will tell you what you need to know."

Rocking on the heel of his chair, James watched as she spoke and wondered what she could have to offer them. After a few minutes, all the officers left the room without saying anything to Sarah.

Outside the door James' heart was beating fast. He wanted to hear her out; he also knew he had complicated his own investigation into catching Snake.

Sarah, sitting behind the cold metal desk, smiled at him when he returned. Looking directly at him, she said, "Lover-boy Johnny, do your buddies know about you and me? Or should I tell them myself?"

James feeling uncomfortable began sweating. Leaning across the table and looking straight at her, he said, "Listen Sarah, yes our paths have crossed in the past but right now, we are talking about you and the fact your action got two men killed. Let us not lose focus on the fact, you are working for Snake. My advice to you is to start talking and you better give us relevant information as nothing else matters at this time."

The other officers slowly returned their focus to Sarah; waiting for her to begin speaking. They also had silly grins; thinking about the possible story behind him and Sarah's relationship.

Sighing deeply, she knew she had played her last card and her little secret was of no value anymore.

For the hour, she spoke of her business connections but provided limited information about Lucas.

"What's the connection between you and Snake? Are you his woman?"

Baring her teeth, she laugh and looking directly at him, asked, "Do you think I am? You must be dreaming or something. I have nothing more to say to you. I will speak with my lawyer."

Soon her lawyer arrived and bailed her out. James objected to any bail and strongly voiced his concerns, but the Justice of the Peace eventually set her bail at $100,000 with strict conditions including the surrendering of her passport and placed on electronic monitoring. Shortly after, she strolled out of the Police Station hanging on to the lawyer's arms, never taking a second look behind her.

Upset, James knew there was nothing he could do to prevent her from being released. He had to find another way to stop her and Snake.

James speaking privately with Shane, told him about the officer's action. For the next while, they both check out all the companies named by Sarah, looking for a connection between Snake and herself; they would not give up.

After cross referencing all the companies, they found three names kept reoccurring and James made note of each. He had Shane check them in more detail with the intention of visiting the identified locations.

Sergeant Harris called James as he was about to leave the squad-room. "How are things going Jim, do you have everything under control?"

"What do you mean, work wise or?"

"I am sure if things at home weren't going well, you know I would probably hear about it from your sister-in-law. No, I am speaking about your investigation on Snake. I understand you had some other run-in with this young woman we arrested."

"Ah Paul, she is the contact I was working with but there is nothing to worry about."

"Well, whatever you do, please don't screw this up."

Waving his hands above his head, he quickly walked out the door and sat at his desk. Long evening shadows lingered against the window panes as he completed the report. Calling at day, he got into his car and drove home.

` ` `

Bini now upset with Sarah; was afraid to ask her how much information she had shared with the police but needed to know

"Exactly what did you tell the cops in there and why didn't you call me as soon as you got to the station?"

Flashing her hair aside, she said, "I told them nothing to make them any wiser to Lucas or even about you. You should have some faith in me."

"Ok, I want to believe you but I am worried. Two of our men are dead and Lucas will not like it. This is no longer business as usual, we need to be smart with whatever we do from here on out," he replied.

Bini was thinking he had to start following her as she could no longer be trusted. She appeared too cautious in speaking with him about her interactions with the police. He was also concerned as he had not heard anything from his police source for some time.

` ` `

Shane seated on a stool in the bar, having a drink at the Condor, on the west side of the city. It had been more than two weeks since the shooting and he still found it difficult to move on. After speaking with the Police psychiatrist, he was still experiencing nightmares. Late in the night and on his second drink, the distinct footsteps of a female caught his ears.

Sliding next to him, she ordered a drink but he never bothered to look in her direction. He was in a world of his own and caught up in his own thoughts when he heard the stranger say.

"Hello there, mind if I join you for awhile? You don't mind some company?"

Slowly turning around, he finally looked and smiling, he saw a set of the darkest brown eyes he had even seen.

"It depends on who is asking and what kind of company you are offering," he replied.

"Hi, I'm Greta and I don't enjoy drinking alone. You look like you could do with some company. Please don't feel pressured because I ask you. Are you alone?" she said as she extended her right hand.

"I am Harry and yes I am on my own."

"No girlfriend or wife waiting at home for you, Harry?"

"Sorry, none of the above, and what about you, do you a boyfriend?"

"No, I don't. My family and I recently moved from another city. I was offered a teaching position here in town."

Greta was 25 years old and lived with her parents and an older brother.

Shane took his time looking at her as she continued to tell him about herself. She looked a lot younger than her stated age with youthful features.

"I live in the area and work as a sales clerk down at the hardware store," he said.

"You certainly do not look like any store clerk I have seen. Are you sure you are not fibbing?"

Smiling, he never answered and continued to sip his drink. He kept staring at her with an inquisitive look. She was quick to notice him smiling and wondered what he could possibly be smiling about.

As the drinks flowed, their inhibitions loosened and eventually, he said, "Actually, I'm a Police man; I don't work at the hardware store."

As soon as he said it, he regretted it as he had promised himself not to let on as to his profession. It was too late as he noticed the surprised look on her face. His face flushed, he wasn't sure how she would take this information.

He waited for her to freak out or react in some strange way but she didn't. Feeling more at ease, and taking a deep breath, he said, "Also, my name not is Harry but Shane."

"I thought you looked more like a cop than a clerk but why did you say you were a store clerk and named Harry? You are not hiding anything else are you? By the way, you are kind of cute too. "

Smiling, he replied, "Thank you, anyway, some people aren't comfortable speaking with a cop so I don't like telling people about my job or my real name. You would eventually find out so I figure I would tell you now."

As the bar closed, they walked out together; still chatting like old friends.

"Would you like to see me sometimes?"

"Yes, Greta, I would love."

As they reached her car, Greta kissed him on the cheek and smiled and got inside. Sitting for a moment, she called out to him, "Hey Shane, can you drive me home? I'm a tipsy and would rather not drive. I could get my car tomorrow."

Chuckling, he said, "I would be happy to take you home."

Soon, they arrived at her house and he pulling in to the driveway, he watched as she walked to her door.

Pulling away, he was lost in the music on the radio. Along the way, he never saw the car bearing down on him until it was too late. Swerving to his right, he watched the car passed by mere inches from him.

Settling his nerves, he turned his car around and continued oh his journey. There would not be any further sighting of this car.

Lying in bed, thoughts of Greta returned and he held his pillows close and dozed off.

Beneath her covers, Greta spent the next half an hour reminiscing about the past evening with Shane. She loved her brother and was hurt for him when his marriage broke down. She had become close to his wife and shared many pleasant times with her. As such she was cautious about getting involved but meeting Shane caused her to begin to think maybe, things could be different.

Sleep was difficult for Shane as in the wee hours; he woke up with sweat running down body. He saw men chasing both Greta and him across an open field with nowhere to hide. Running as fast as they both could, they were unable to get away. As the men closed in, he woke up with his heart pounding.

Taking deep breaths, he tried to understand the dream and attributed it to a combination of the past shoot-out and meeting her last evening. Shaking his head, he got up and poured himself a glass of water.

He wondered how she felt about him. The warm feeling he had when they embraced came back to him and he chuckled. He would wait for a few days before contacting her; he didn't want to appear to be too anxious.

` ` `

Standing inches from Sarah's face, Lucas screamed at her, "How could you be so darn careless to have Ed and Tom killed and getting yourself arrested? I thought you were smart. Why didn't you work with Bini? You know he should be the one to plan this."

"Listen honey, I spoke with him and he was comfortable with the plan, I don't know how the policeman got away. What happened to our guy on the inside?"

Throwing an ashtray across the desk, he said, "The stupid fart got himself caught sending me a message right in front the other cops. Now he is out on his ass, now he is of no use to us. For Christ sake! I can't believe Ed and Tom are gone, all because of your carelessness, you will have to go away for a while."

"Where would you suggest I go, Lucas, they have my passport and you had to post my bond?"

"I don't care about the money. We need to get you out of the country to a place that does not have an extradition agreement with us."

"What about us, where do we stand? Will we ever be together again?"

"Look, don't worry; you know I have the ability to travel anywhere. Once things settle down, I will join you; my business associates will continue to manage my affairs here."

Feeling abandoned, she found difficult to deal with. Seeing her already afoul of the law, she figured she could not do any worse and so she began her ideas in motion.

Chapter 8

"Bini, come and see me now, I need to have a few words with you," said Lucas on the other end of the call.

"Can we do it over the phone, I kind of have a situation here," Bini replied.

"Are you refusing to see me? I need to see you in person and you better be here within the next fifteen minutes."

Shaking, Bini had never heard Lucas speak to him in that manner before. He knew he could not avoid answering to Lucas. Ten minutes later, he timidly walked down the dark corridor of the bar, his stomach in a knot; his boss wasn't someone to cross or fail to follow his order.

Stepping inside the dimly lit room, he saw Lucas sitting at the head of a long table. Beside him were two other men he had never seen before.

Nervously, he looked around and wondered if this was where his life would end. The door slamming behind jolted him and he was frisked by yet another unknown male. Snatching his gun, the man laid it on the desk.

Cold sweat ran down his back as he sat at the other end of the table. With wobbling knees, he kept his eyes on Lucas and the two men beside him.

"Bini, I am beginning to think you are not the man for the job. I told you to keep an eye on Sarah and her coming and going and so far you have failed. First we lost a shipment of guns at the warehouse, had our men shot up and now we have lost two of our best guys. What exactly is happening?"

"Well, I don't know how the warehouse was raided. It' far out of the way and Sarah told me she had things under control in respect to the cop. She made all the plans and assured me she was capable of seeing it through."

"Bini, Bini, why do I give you all these perks when you are not doing what I need you to do. You aren't useful anymore."

Squirming in the chair, he watched one of the men sitting near Lucas toying with his gun. Things weren't looking good for him and he could not see any way out.

"Boss, I will make it happen, just give me another chance."

"I think it's a little too late, your promises don't have much weight to me right now.

The man behind Bini slipped a plastic bag over his face and tightened it. Choking, he clawed at the empty space as his breath was sucked out of him.

The knock on the door frightened everyone and the man behind him looked at Lucas.

"Release him. Who is it; I thought I said I shouldn't be disturbed whenever I am working?"

"Lucas, it's me Henry. I am in the area and wanted to say a quick hello, I won't be long."

As the bag was pulled off his head, Bini fell to the floor gasping for air. He knew he was on the wrong side of Lucas and he had to start looking out for himself.

"Today is your lucky day, get out of here. I will be watching you and if this cop continues to be a problem, remember, you will be next. No one will save you, mark my words."

With wobbling legs, Bini stumbled out the door as Henry walked in; never taking a second look at him. Henry knew enough about the nature of Lucas' work not to be too alarmed. In fact, they were two of a kind and not surprised by anything he did.

Finding his strength, Bini made a fast exit and raced to his car. Once inside, he secured the doors and screamed. He knew had he not gone as ordered; he probably would have not survived. Now he had to find Sarah, she was responsible for all of this.

``` ` ` ` ```

Sitting at home in her lounge wear, Sarah was pining for James even though he no longer had any interested in her. Lucas was her partner but he didn't make her feel the way James did. She wanted him and was willing to break all rules to have him once more even after trying to have him killed.

The ringing of the door bell broke her thoughts. Slipping on her robe, she walked to the front-door. Peering through the peep-hole, she saw Bini and was taken aback.

"Lucas is not here, you know he never does any business here. What is it
```

you want?" she asked.

Banging on the door, he said, "I need to speak with you; can you please open the door for me? I don't want to talk to you through a closed door."

Slightly opening the door, she glanced at him and noted how red his face. Before she could ask him about his face, he quickly forced his way inside. Once inside, he placed his hands across her mouth and pulled her down onto the floor. Eventually he removed his hand from her mouth once she promised not to scream.

"What the hell is wrong with you? Have you gone freaking mad and were you trying to kill me?"

"Your boyfriend almost killed me because of your failure."

"So you are going to kill me because of that, what do you think Lucas will do to you? If you think what he did was bad, I can assure you he would make you pa. I suggest you leave now and I will pretend this never happened."

"Sarah, I came here with the intent to get even with you for making my life hell but now I am thinking otherwise. We know Lucas wants the cop out of the way as he has caused him some headache. What if you and I put our heads together and get this guy once for all? Lucas would be happy with both of us. What do you have to say? You know how to reach this guy, don't you?"

Staring at him, she said, "Yeah, I know how to reach him but have you forgotten he arrested me. I don't want to get in any deeper trouble with the Police; I have had my share for now, thank you much."

"No Sarah, you and I are going to do this, one way or the other, my life is on the line and I know you can help. Have you forgotten all the times I helped you? We both need to do this."

"Ok Bini, we will do it together," she said not too convincing.

"What the hell are you doing in my house and what are you two doing? Bini, you are lucky Henry came when he did. If you know what's good for you, get out of here while you can."

Jumping up and facing Lucas, Bini said, "We were talking about the cop. We are going to get the son of a bitch, I promise."

"Ok Bini, you have one more chance to prove yourself. Get this done or this will be your last go-around," he said while shoving him through the door.

Outside the door, he heard Lucas shouting at Sarah.

"Are you having an affair with him and why he was there?"

Cozying up to him and wrapping her arms around him, she said, "Why would I? Seeing you provide us with everything we need? I don't want anyone but you honey, why don't we go to the bedroom? It's been a long time since we spend some quality time together."

Bini knew his days were numbered; by the way Lucas looked at him. He knew he was on his own in more ways than one; Sarah would never betray Lucas. He had to find a way to get to her and force her to stick with him.

` ` `

Greta sat in her room, excited yet worried; having looked at a number of apartments she could afford. Now she wanted to go live on her own.

Having a close-knit family, she wasn't sure what they would say about it. Building up the courage, she eventually walked out of her room and sat down with her parents and brother.

Hugging herself; she cleared her throat and began; "Now you guys know I have a job here and I will be making a good salary, right?"

Her father was the first to speak, "Greta, what is it you are so afraid to tell us, come on, let's hear it."

Turning to look directly at him, she said, "Well dad, I am thinking of moving on my own. I think it's time I start trying to make a life for myself."

"Why, this is so sudden my dear. Is it something we did or say? You know you don't have to go, we are both happy to have you and your brother home with us," said her mom.

"I know mom, but I would like to see if I can make it on my own. Look at David, he tried and so I would like to do the same."

"Is there any other reason Greta? You know, we understand your need for independence but also want to make sure you are making this decision for the correct reason," her father asked with a smile.

"Dad, I have met a young man, yes, but it's not the reason. I want to give you some space as I feel having David and me here can be stressful at times."

"So Greta, when do you plan to move and have you found a place as yet," ask her dad.

"Right now, I am looking at a few places and I hope to select the one I like and can afford."

"Maybe your mom could go with you in your search and maybe, we might get to meet this young man? Listen my dear, we are supportive of any decision you make as we know you will make the right one," said her dad.

"So tell us about this young man, what is he like and what does he do for a living?" ask David.

"Well, it's not because of him as we recently met. He is a Policeman in town and around my age. He is quite nice and a gentleman; he drove me home the other night."

Walking by her side, her mother held her close, "That's so lovely, you remind me of when your dad and I met. I would be happy to help you look for an apartment and maybe we will get to meet this young man if you think you both are going to develop a relationship."

"Sis, I am happy for you and you know I will be there for you always."

Grinning, Greta hugged each as she expected some resistance. She was prepared for a battle in trying convincing them but it never materialized.

Shane was also thinking of her and after their last conversation, he felt there might be a connection between them. He wanted to see if they could take it further. It had been a few days since they last spoke but he didn't want to rush into anything.

His last girlfriend was Wendy, a high school experience which never developed into anything serious. At the end of their junior years, she moved away and there was no further contact.

In fact he was thinking to ask Det. Williams for some advice. He felt the detective would not laugh at him for asking certain questions.

` ` `

Driving the long way home, James had time to reflect on the past events, things were becoming uncomfortable. His boss, his wife's brother-in-law and fellow officers knew enough about his possible involvement with Sarah. It might be only a matter of time before things get back to Bev. He couldn't afford to lose her and the children and he knew he certainly would.

Finally at home, even though he felt a bit wound-up, he needed to hold Bev; she was his security blanket. After a quick shower, he joined her in bed and as she pulled him close, he no longer was thinking about anyone or anything else except her.

He rose late the next day and sat on the bed as sunlight peeked through the window blinds. Smiling, he watched Bev still lying in bed.

"Are you ok honey?" she asked as she pressed herself close to him. She felt warm and soft and he was tempted to get back in the bed but he had other things on his mind

"Everything is fine, I'm a bit tired but I will be ok after a quick shower."

After sometime, he stepped from bathroom and strolled into the kitchen. Bev was already preparing breakfast and the scent of ackee and codfish filtered through the doors. She handed him a cup of black coffee and as he sat down, he began to scan the morning paper.

The vibration of his cell signaled a call was coming in. He chose to ignore it; he was with his family. Three more calls came through within an hour and while he tried to ignore them, curiosity got the better of him.

Stepping into the family room, he returned the call, "Sarah, what do you want; don't you think you are in enough trouble as it is?"

"I know, Johnny, but I can't help it and I am sorry."

"Being sorry right now does not make any difference; it's too late."

"Please wait a minute, can I explain? Don't hang up, not yet."

"Alright Sarah, I'm listening and you have two minutes."

"When we first met, I didn't know of your interest in Lucas, right? I liked you for being you. When you asked me about him, I got caught between my feelings for you and what I was told to do."

"So, are you now admitting to knowing Snake?"

"Yes, I know him but if I were to tell you about him would be like me signing my own death warrant."

"Goodbye Sarah, you have made your choice and now have time to think about what you will tell the judge. You and I have nothing more to say to each other, bye."

"Johnny, can you see me one more time? I promise you, I won't try anything. My life is already in a mess, I don't want to make it any worse, please meet me tomorrow, and let's say, around noon at Sam's cafe?"

"Look, I can't be seen with you. I will try to be there however if you don't see me you know why, as I do not trust you, goodbye."

"Who was it dear?" Bev asked.

"Oh, it was one of my street contacts wanting to meet with me tomorrow, looking for a favor."

Shaking her head, she thought there was too much of a familiarity in the way he spoke and it caused her some concerns.

Chapter 9

Late in the evening, James visited an old abandoned construction site now a hang-out place for several street-people.

This part of the city politicians had completely forgotten about. There was tall grass growing in and around them.

Coming up the rough road, he saw a man staggering out of one of the buildings and bleeding from the head. Braking quickly, he jumped out and while cradling him, called for assistance.

The paramedics arrived within a few minutes and began to provide assistance to the injured. James wanting to learn what had happened to this man parked and began to move towards the group watching from afar.

Trying to gather information about the injured man proved futile. As he turned to walk away, he heard, "Psst, over here."

Looking over his shoulder, he saw someone hiding behind a half wall. Circling the broken-down building, he came up behind the person and offered the man a smoke.

"Do you know the man and what may have happened?"

"Yeah, I know him as Stan and they accused of trying to steal from the guy you see standing there in the torn black pants and sleeveless shirt."

James said, "Do you think he did stole anything and by the way, what's your name?"

"Ah, you can call me Peter and I don't know. Look, I have to be careful as I don't want them to think I am a snitch. Down here, you can't trust anyone."

"Ok Peter, I understand, here are a few bucks and may I come by another time and ask you some more questions, how long have you been living on the streets?"

"I have been homeless for the past six months. If you wish, I could meet you somewhere else if you tell me where."

"Alright, I will be at 5th and West Street between six and seven tomorrow evening if you can meet me there."

"You are a cop, right?"

James' eyes widened at the question and chuckling, he said, "Why do you think so? I am looking for someone I think is living on the streets."

"You look like a cop and the way you ask questions."

"No, I am not a cop but if I were, would you still be willing to speak with me?

"Sure, I don't have anything against cops but the others might have different opinions."

"Ok, I hear you, see you if you can make it," and James cautiously walked back to his car.

Arriving at the hospital, James located the injured man's room and while walking towards it, was stopped by a nurse.

"Sorry, you can't see the patient at this time; he is unconscious and we are not allowing anyone to see him."

Flashing his badge, he said, "I am the officer who called tried to help the injured man."

"Ok, a few minutes, but he won't be able to speak with you."

Stepping into the room, James was taken aback by the number to tubes inserted in the injured man; he was hardly breathing. He turned and walked away.

At the nurses' desk, he handed them his card and said, "Should there be any improvement in his condition, kindly give me call at this number."

"Officer, before you go, may I have a word with you?" asked the head nurse.

Staring at her name tag, he noticed her name; Candy Button,

"Sure Nurse Button, what would you like to know?"

Smiling broadly, she looked into his eyes, "How did you know my name?"

Pointing to her name tag, James smiled at her.

"I am sorry, officer, my bad. Will you be back?" she asked.

"I am not sure, Nurse Button, why do you ask?"

Lowering her stare, she said, "Please call me Candy, I would love to ask you some questions."

"Candy, are you ..?" he asked.

With a sly smile, she replied, "Maybe I am."

"Well now, let's see, if his situation changes in any way, why don't you give me call," James said as he walked away.

He felt her eyes following him and he chuckled as he too had made a mental note of her. She was an attractive woman beneath all her nurse's outfit.

` ` `

At the station, Shane was giddy with a wide smile

Tapping him on the shoulder, James asked, "What's happening with you?"

Pretending not to know what he was speaking about, "Nothing is happening."

"Come on Shane, everyone can see something is going on. Why don't you spill it out, you know you want to."

"All right, I have met a young woman and we seem to hit it off."

"Well, sounds wonderful and it might be a good thing for you. Make sure to take your time; don't go rushing into anything too heavy until you are sure. Have you ever had a girlfriend before?"

"Not anything serious, once while in high school but it wasn't a big thing so I am a little nervous. You have been married for a long time, haven't you, what other advice would you give me?"

"Tell me a little about this young lady. Where did you meet and how long have you known her?"

"I met her a few nights ago while hanging out at a bar and she is real nice."

"First, you should go on a real date, something you plan and see how much you both have in common. Make sure you both share some interests and goals.

"Yes, that's what life is all about. Life with a partner can be wonderful but it takes time and hard work you both must be willing to put in it," he continued.

"Thanks, Det. I think I will call her after a few days and see how it goes."

` ` `

Greta was feeling light-headed as she danced around her bedroom. She planned to go into town and hoped she "accidentally" run into him; she definitely wanted to see him again.

She also wondered how he may have felt about her and would he call her. She decided, should he not call in a few days, she would call. She still wasn't sure if she should tell him she was seeking her own residence as it might frighten him away.

She wondered out loud, "What if he did not find me attractive and only said he would call me to be polite?"

The thought frightened her to the point her heart began to race and she had to sit down. She kept telling herself he must have liked her and she should not think otherwise.

` ` `

James' telephone lit up with up with the in-coming call. He reached for it and the voice on the other end said, "Det. Williams? This is Nurse Candy Buttons. I want to give you an update about the gentleman who came in last night."

"Yes, this is Det. Williams. What's the update?"

"Unfortunately, he passed away from his injuries and we thought you wanted to know, sorry."

"Thanks for the update, Nurse Buttons. Were you able to find out if he had any family members in this area?"

"Sorry Det. we were never able to speak with him, we tried our best but the doctors couldn't save him. Do you plan on coming by anytime soon?"

"OK, Candy, I can swing by in a little while and speak with you."

Her soft voice was noticed by James and it actually turned him on. Leaning back in his chair he smiled as he thought about the possibilities.

Looking at his watch, he noticed it was mid-day but he had no intention of meeting Sarah. He would rather visit the hospital and speak with Nurse Button. He believed it was more than talking about the deceased.

With a spring in her steps, Nurse Button kept busy, knowing James would soon be visiting.

"What has come over you?" her co-worker asked.

"Why? Nothing at all, I'm in a happy mood."

Shortly after, James arrived and found his way to the nurses' desk where Candy was waiting for him.

"Would you like to take a walk to the cafeteria with me Det. Williams? There we can talk without all the noise you hear up here."

"Sure, I have a few minutes to spare and feel free to call me James seeing you have insisted I call you Candy. Lead the way and we can talk while we walk."

"I guess as a policeman you see and hear all kinds of things, don't you, James?"

"Yes but I could also say the same to you, as I am sure you see a lot worse than we do. How long have you been a nurse?"

"Well, for fifteen years and at this hospital for the past nine years but funny enough, I have seen many other officers here but not you."

Finding an empty table, they sat down, facing each other.

"It has been many years since I last worked one. But tell me Candy, I think there's more to you asking me to meet with you. If we wanted to speak about the deceased, we could have done it over the phone."

Looking down and without saying a word, she reached across the table for his hand. Turning his palm in the air, she began to stroke it; going in small circles with her fingernails.

"Ok, but do tell me, why me?"

"I don't actually know Jay, when I first saw you, a feeling I am still unable to explain came over me. I hope maybe you would be interested too. I am sorry if I am mistaken; you don't have to say anything if you are not interested, I won't feel offended."

Placing his hand on her hand, he said, "Well, I could be but don't you think we should get to know each other first? For one thing, I am married with children and don't have any plan or interest in leaving my family."

"Oh, maybe an occasional get together if it's something you would consider. Also, I am single with no children and have my own house so there would not be any concerns on my part."

"Ok, why don't we meet for a late lunch one afternoon when we are both available and see how it goes?"

"That would be fantastic, here is my private number, and you may call me anytime unless I am working. Sorry if I came on too strong or scared you for being too upfront."

"Not at all, I like a woman who is upfront; at least we both know where each one stands. Anyway, I must be going as this report will not complete itself."

"Oh yes, I had almost forgotten, the paper work has been completed, let's go back and I will retrieve it for you."

With the document in hand, he walked away from her desk feeling almost like a young kid in a candy store.

` ` `

Sarah sat motionless in her car, waiting for James to appear. This time she was alone with the electronic monitoring bracelet strapped on her left ankle. While massaging her ankle, she searched the area with a hope of glimpsing him. It wasn't to be and so she resigned to the fact he wouldn't be coming.

Questioning her instinct, she thought she had won him over and he still had feelings for her. She had to find another way to get him to meet her and so she slowly pulled away from the curb.

Bini parked a few meters behind Sarah and watched her leaving. "Another failed attempt on your part," he snickered under his breath.

He knew Lucas would keep his word and killing him would be no big deal. Lucas had no loyalty to anyone but himself. Bini would follow her and see what she was up to next.

He wondered if he would be able to find his own men, form his own gang and eventually get to Lucas before he got him. He also knew if it were to happen, it had to be now as he did not have much time.

` ` `

Thinking about Sarah, James figured she must be long gone once she realized he wasn't going to meet her. He eventually arrived at the planned location and she was long gone, so he headed for the station.

Pulling into the Police parking lot, he saw several officers walking quite swiftly. Shouting at one of the officers, he asked, "Why everyone is in such haste?"

"Didn't you hear? Sgt. James collapsed and is getting medical attention in the sick bay."

"What the hell, how did it happen?" said James as he too rushed into the building.

Once inside, he found Sgt. Harris, sitting in a chair with an oxygen mask on.

"Are you ok Paul, what happened? You scared the hell out of all of us as you can see."

Looking around the room, Sgt. Harris said, "I am ok, it's due to the heat. Trust me, I'll be fine."

As he spoke, the officers slowly walked out of the room and left him alone with James.

"Man, you scared me to hell. Should I call Mary?"

"Hell no, you can't tell her. You know she has been asking me about cutting back on the job? This would only give her more ammunition and I am not ready for that right now."

James began to laugh out loudly.

"What's so funny Jim?"

"I am not laughing at you at all. It's the same conversation Bev and I were having a few days ago. You think both sisters were talking to each other about this?"

"One never knows but right now you can't say anything to Mary or even Bev as you know the other will certainly hear about it."

Soon it was time for James to meet Peter. This time, he would travel alone without Shane; he didn't want to scare Peter seeing he already thought he was a cop.

Arriving at 3rd and West Street, he parked out of the way and waited. It wasn't too long before he saw Peter looking around and honking his horn, James signaled him over. Peter walked pass the car some ways before returning and getting into the passenger's seat.

"I know you are a cop but it's ok, I don't mind speaking with you."

"Glad to know you are ok speaking to me, Peter and yes, I am a police officer. What else do you remember about the fight between Stan and the other man? Is he still down at the old buildings and what is his name?"

"Most persons there don't give their real names but I hear others call him Patrick and yes he is there when I left today. I heard Stan might have been stealing his drugs but that's all I know."

"Do you know where he is getting his stuff from, like a dealer?"

"There is this guy, I don't know his name but he comes around once every two or three weeks. He never gets out of his car but he would have his driver hand Patrick a parcel."

"And you have never seen this person. Do they share any with you?"

"I have glimpsed him once and he is kind of dark skin and I think he is partially bald. He is a bit flashy as his car is an expensive European car, you know, it looks like a bimmer but I am not too sure."

"When was the last time he came around?"

"Oh, I thought you were interested in what happened to Stan?" asked Peter.

"Yes, I am interested in what happened to Stan. This I can share with you, Stan passed away from his injuries last night."

"Gosh, I am sorry, he never bothered anyone."

"So you see, if someone provided the drugs which may have indirectly caused his death, I would like to know more about the supplier," James replied.

"I think he came by about two weeks ago, can't say for sure."

"Ok, here's what I want you to do for me. I will send some officers to pick up Patrick tomorrow and I want you to be there. You need to stay out of the way, make sure the others see you. I don't want them to think you had anything to do with it, understand?"

"Ok, I can do that. Anything else you want me to do?"

"That's good enough for now unless you know for sure when next this person will be coming by. Here is my card and a few bucks. Make sure to put it away, remember, you can't afford for them to even think you know anything about this."

Turning over the card, Peter eyes brightened. "You know, I have a good friend who mentioned your name. His name is Rick and he said you were the only cop he ever trusted, wow, fancy my meeting you."

"Yes, I helped him out once. Can I trust you Peter?"

"No problem Det. Williams, Rick and I are close and I think I am the only one he told."

Chapter 10

At the station, James called the staff together, "I will be going under cover tonight. At day break you need to pick up anyone who fails to give their names; me included. Here is the address."

Reaching for his phone, he called Bev, "Honey, please don't wait up for me tonight, I have to do something which will keep me busy for rest of the night."

"Is everything ok, Jimmy, you are not hanging out with the guys playing cards or dominoes, are you?"

"No, nothing like that at all, I will fill you in when I get home, nothing to worry about my love, it's all part of the job."

"Ok, whatever you do, please be careful and I love you," she replied.

"Love you too dear, see you later."

Sliding into her comfortable chair, Bev thought about what he had said. She wanted to think he would not do anything to hurt her but she could not help thinking about what he might be doing on such a night.

She considered visiting the station but was afraid of what she might find out if he wasn't actually working. Eventually, she decided against following up on her plan and hoped for the best.

As darkness covered the city, James pulled away from the station and headed towards the run-down buildings. He soon found a safe place to park; some distance from the intended location.

From the car trunk, he pulled out a disguise and spent the next half an hour putting it on. On his back was an old sack with tattered clothes, a few sticks of marijuana, bedding and some ready to eat canned food. Upon his head, he had long dirty matted dread locks wig and his face smeared with paint.

Walking slowly with a hunch back and assisted by a cane, he soon came upon the group.

Without looking at anyone in particular; he kept on walking until he found an available spot and sat down. Somewhere behind him, he heard a screaming voice, "Hey you, what are you doing down here? We have never seen you here before."

As the crowd got closer, he searched for Patrick but he wasn't there and he felt disappointed.

Soon the crowd parted as a tall figure walked towards him. With the moon shining behind the man, James found it difficult to see his face until they were a few inches from each other.

"What the hell do you want down here; did you lose your way? We don't get many strangers down here, who are you?" said Patrick.

"I am Ed and I'm looking a place to stay for the night, don't mean any harm. I will stay out of your way and will be gone by daybreak," said James, relieved to see Patrick.

"I have some goodies, if you want," he continued.

Snatching the bag from him, Patrick ripped it open and threw the contents on the ground. Finding the marijuana, he picked it up, kicked the other contents aside and walked away.

James watched as the others followed him; all except one person; it was Peter.

For a moment his heart skipped a beat when he saw Peter standing there but he never recognized him.

"Sorry, old man, he is a bully and we are all avoiding him. He can be an ass especially when he smokes. Do you want me to help gather up your things?" said Peter.

James replied, "No, it is ok, I will be here for the night and I will be gone but thanks for the offer."

"It doesn't matter that I don't know you, we are all in the same boat otherwise you and I wouldn't be down here. By the way, I am Pete."

"Glad to meet you Pete, you feel safe down here with these guys?"

"Yes, they don't bother me and I stay out of the way plus being the youngest here, they always have me running errands for them."

"Like what errands if you don't mind my asking you?"

"Oh for food and kind of being a look-out for others who might come and steal our stuff. You will be safe here for tonight now he has your stuff. He will soon pass out."

For the rest of the night, James stayed close to his spot as he kept an eye on Patrick.

The Police officers moved in as the sun was rising and quickly rounded up everyone including James. Lining them all up against a wall, the Police questioned each. Most provided the requested information except Patrick, James and two others. As a result, the four of them were taken into custody and placed in the paddy-wagon.

Sitting in the back of the wagon, James looked at Patrick and the other men but only Patrick appeared worried.

"Hey man, why you look so worried? They will release us once we get there. They only wanted to know who we are and I don't like cops so I never give them my name," said James.

"I don't have any problem with them but I still get nervous around them. Someone came around here the other day when someone got hurt. He was asking all kinds of questions. People think I did it," Patrick replied.

"And did you, did you hurt this person?" asked James.

"Why are you asking me? I already told them I didn't do anything to him. Look I am sorry about the way I came onto you last night, we get nervous when strangers come around but I didn't mean you any harm."

Leaning against door, James said, "Not to worry, I didn't take it personal, I was looking for a place to rest for the night and now here I am sitting with you in this paddy-wagon."

At the station, Patrick and the other chaps were placed in a holding cell while James was taken to another interview room.

"You fooled them for sure Det. Williams, good disguise," said Shane.

"You know, I was worried as my contact was there but fortunately, even he did not recognize me. We will deal with Patrick later, right now, I am heading home."

` ` `

While driving home, James had the window down and the cool summer breeze engulfed the cabin. On the radio, the song "Case you didn't know" played softly in the background and it brought thoughts of Bev. The thought of her not being there scared him more than he would admit.

Coming through the door, he reached for her and she willingly slid into his arms and held him tight.

"I love you Bev and don't know what I would do without you."

"Jimmy, what has come over you this morning?"

"Nothing my dear, lately I have not taken the time to tell you how much I love and appreciate you and think it's time I start doing."

"Wow, I am happy to hear you say it and yes you have been taking some things for granted but I'm glad to know you appreciate me. I must be honest with you though," Walking away, she continued. "Last night when you called, I thought of coming to the station to see if you were working. Don't ask me why, I felt a bit uncomfortable and all kinds of thoughts crossed my mind."

Hearing this, his eyes opened wide and for a moment, he was unable to speak. Finally, he said, "Now why were you thinking that way, have I ever given you reason not to trust me?"

"Jimmy, no, you have not but at times, I do wonder whenever you come home and having that funky smell, it does cause me to wonder, sorry."

Pulling her close to him, he said, "I promised to share more information about the previous night with you. Now I do need a shower."

After showering, he took his time to gather his thoughts before joining the family for breakfast. After breakfast he laid it all out to Bev, all the events of the last evening. He kept assuring her, his safety was never in question.

She didn't flinch on the outside as she didn't want him to see her fear for him; inside, she was a mess but knew she had to hold it together.

"I am sorry for doubting you about last night."

Holding her tight, he whispered, "I understand your concerns but there is nothing to worry about."

Once the house became quiet, he retired to the bedroom and slept like a baby for a few hours only to wake up by the sound of the alarm. He had enough time to get himself a snack and get the children before heading off to work.

John and Sharon were on time and happy to see their dad but Dudley not at the agreed meeting place.

"Guys, where is your brother, and why is it he always s to be so tardy?"

John was the first to speak, "Dad, I think he has a girlfriend and maybe they are hanging out. Do you want me to go and look for him?"

"Yes, John, please go and look for him and tell him to hurry as I need to get to work. I will need to have a serious conversation with him."

James could hear Sharon snickering in the backseat and with a smile ask her, "What's so funny pumpkin?"

"John has a girlfriend and he is going to get into trouble."

"No, he won't be in any trouble at all. We need him to be a bit more responsible. You all know your mom and my schedule and we all have deadlines and rules to be followed."

Soon John and Dudley returned and Dudley giving his dad a half of an excuse as to why he was late.

"Save it Dudley, your brother and sister already told me why. So who is she and how come your mother and I haven't heard of her?"

"You guys told him?" shouted Dudley.

"It's ok Dudley; you need to be more responsible when it comes to meeting our schedule. You know the routine, today your mom dropped you off and I come to get you before I go off to work. Maybe it's time we allow you to come home on your own, seeing you are now thirteen years old. When I get home later, we will discuss it with your mom and see what she says."

Dudley had a big smile on his face and nudged his siblings with his elbows. Eventually he responded with a weak, "yes dad."

Soon, they arrived at home and after briefly speaking with Bev, James went on his way to work; they would talk about Dudley later.

` ` `

As James travelled along the busy hi-way, he realized he had some time to kill and so he decided to visit up an old friend. Turning off the hi-way, he arrived at a small high rise building, walked up to the intercom and pressed the buzzer.

On the other side of the intercom he could hear the familiar growl of his of friend, Jack, "Who is it?"

"Hi Jack, it's me, James, can I come up?"

"Sure, hold on a minute."

James hurried up the stairs to the second floor; no time to wait for the elevator, he would get there quicker than waiting for it. He was about to knock on the door when Jack opened it and greeted him with a bear-hug.

"It's good to see you my friend, it has been awhile since we last saw each other. What's been happening with you and how is the family?" asked Jack.

"Man, life has been good, wife and kids are great but the job as you know can be stressful to say the least. What about you my friend, what have you been up to?"

"It's as you see it, not much going on. Not sure if you heard but I had to retire late last year due an accident on the job but no worries, I am fine. So what brings you to my neck of the woods?"

"I was passing your area and remembered, we haven't seen each other for sometime so, here I am."

"Are you sure everything is ok? I can see some stress on your face. You want a drink and maybe you can tell me about it, ok?"

James and Jack had a long history, back when they were kids living on the same block. While they didn't always hang out e day, they shared a number of interests. They were both rough and tumble kids from the wrong side of town who shared a love for sport activities, having an alcoholic drink and of course, women.

Slumping in the comfy chair, James took the drink and began to relate his interaction with Sarah and now Candy. He was quick to admit he had the choice of turning them down and as he didn't, he must take responsibility for his actions.

Jack listened intently without saying a word until he finished, "Well Jim, my boy, the way I see it and you know I am going to be honest with you, right? You love women too much so you find it difficult to refuse any of their advances. But tell me, how does it affect your relationship with Bev, any lack of interest on the home front?"

"Hell no, things there are good, but sometimes I sense she might feels something is not the same," James said with a sheepish look.

"My friend, I noticed you said it's good so I am thinking there is still a possibility for it to be great. You don't have much of a choice to make, your home is important to you and while Sarah has gotten under your skin, initially you got caught up with her for the wrong reason," Staring out the window as he continued, "As for Candy you need to be careful as you never know how it will work out. You certainly don't want to get involved with someone who is going to destroy your marriage and even cost you your career."

"I hear you."

"Mark you; I am not sure if I would have acted differently if I were in your position. You always have the foxy ladies falling over you; I wish I had your problem. Seriously though, be careful. I don't want to read about you and some woman's husband getting into a fight," Jack said with a chuckle.

Soon it was time for James to be on his way and thanking Jack for listening to him, agreed to visit more often.

Waving goodbye, Jack said, "Next have a lady friend for me."

Both friends laughed and parted with a brief hug and soon James was out the door.

Jack's words reverberated in his ears; he knew what he had said was the truth. He knew he could not continue this way; he was getting older and slower.

Chapter 11

Patrick looked around the room with its pale white walls, trying his best to see through the darkened window. Soon, Shane and another officer entered the room and sat down in front of him.

"Were you informed of your rights and that you may speak with a lawyer?" asked Shane.

"Why would I need a lawyer? And yes somebody spoke to me about my rights. You can only charge me with obstruction, give me a ticket and let me go."

"Ok, please sign this release to say you decline contacting a lawyer and we will take it from there" said Shane while giving Patrick the form.

"I am not going to sign anything, why should I? What are you guys trying to do to me?"

James then walked in the room and leaning across the table, grabbed Patrick by the collar and pulled him half way over it. With his face a few inches from Patrick he shouted at him, said, "Sign the god damn paper."

Slumping back in the chair, Patrick looked at him, confused, said, "You look vaguely familiar, have we met before? Oh holy shit, you are the guy from last night and they pretended to arrest you along with the rest of us. I am such a fool; I should have seen you were a cop."

"Yes, I'm a cop."

"The way you walked into our place, I should have known and that's why you were asking me all those questions about Stan. Now, I definitely won't sign any paper and I will speak with a lawyer."

"Well, you do have the right to speak with your lawyer however we are going to charge you with assault causing death. Did you know Stan died from his injuries? Shane, go ahead and book him," said James as walked away.

"Wait a minute, I didn't mean to hurt him, I never heard he died, I'm sorry, listen, and don't put me back in the pig-pen of a cell."

"Didn't you say you wanted to speak with a lawyer, have you change your mind? You know anything you say, we will use it as evidence?" asked James.

"Yes, I understand, but I need to tell you what happened, I will sign the form."

After the written confession as completed and signed, James asked, "Where do you get your drugs?"

"I can't say."

"Listen, it can't get any worse for you, right now you actually looking second degree murder so refusing to tell us who your supplier is does not make sense; he or she can't help you right now," James said while standing two feet from him.

"You don't know Snake, ah mean Lucas; he can get to me anywhere I am."

"Did you say his name is Snake?" asked James.

"No, it's a mistake; I don't know anyone called Snake. I can't say if it's the same person," Patrick said.

Leaning over and facing Patrick, James said, "Ok, one last chance for you to do something right, what is the name of your supplier and how does he/she get the drugs to you?"

"You guys are setting me up to get killed in jail if I give you this information."

"If you cooperate with us, we might be able to speak to the judge and see what can be done for you," said James.

"Alright, alright, they call him Snake and yes he comes by ever so often. You guys know I am signing my death warrant, right?"

"Patrick, you are doing the correct thing, we need to take such a person off the streets. If he didn't supply you with the drugs, you probably would not be sitting here right now," said James.

"Det. Williams, please come here for a minute," said Sgt. Harris as he stood in front of his office. Behind closed door, both men sat down for an informal conversation.

"How are you feeling Paul? You scared the hell out of me and all the other guys the other day."

"I am feeling much better Jim but the experience also have caused me to rethink a number of things."

"Like what Paul?"

"Well, like making some changes with work and stuff like, you know."

"Come on Paul, you are still young, you are not considering retiring are you?"

"Not sure what I want to do but you know I told you Mary has been on my case to make some changes so I am thinking right now. You didn't mention anything to Bev about it did you?"

"No, Paul, you asked me not to and I gave you my word. Whatever you do, please take some time to think this through. On another topic, we closed the case on the homeless guy, Stan. The guy we brought in yesterday admitted to it and insisted it was an accident but of course, it has yet to be proven."

"Good for you. What about the case with Snake, any new leads?"

"Well, it's funny but, there might be a connection between this case and Stan. From what I understand, someone like him has been supplying the homeless down there with drugs and I need to follow up and see where it leads us. I need to wrap this up as it is taking a bit too long."

"Ok, but be careful as always. By the way, have you ever considered completing the sergeant's exam and join me here?"

"Are you serious? Not suggesting that what you do isn't important but Paul, you know how I feel about desk work, I enjoy being on the streets. I think I would maybe go crazy if I work indoors all the time, no I haven't given it much thought."

"I guess you know how I feel now, anyway, do think about it as I can put in a word for you; you are a good officer."

"Thanks Paul but you are not saying this because of our wives?"

"Come on Jim, you know me, think about it, won't you?"

"Ok, ok, I will think about it and let you know. We need to get our families together soon. Why not let us ask the wives to arrange it, what do you say?"

Walking away from Paul's office, he shook his head to clear his thoughts; he was thrown when asked about taking the sergeant's exam. He had not given it a thought but now it was put to him, he wondered if he should consider it.

Putting his hand on Shane, he said, "So, how is the girlfriend situation going?"

"Ah, Det. Williams, funny you should ask, there is not much to tell, I have yet to call her, we have been busy. I may give her a call tomorrow."

"Don't wait too long, if she is as nice a person as you said, someone else may also be showing interest in her."

The rising tide of fear flowed through his body, Shane thought about what he said. Picking up the telephone, he dialed her number and waited.

` ` `

Greta, up and about in the town, having decided to move out on her own, she was determined to find an apartment. Moreover if she wanted to develop any relationship, living with her parents might not be a great idea. Once she found something she liked, she would have her mother look at it with her. She still felt the need to do it by herself but also trusted her mother's opinion.

The phone vibrated in her hand and glancing at it saw it was Shane. Her heart beating faster, she didn't want to appear too anxious and so she allowed the message to go to voicemail; she would respond in a few minutes once her excitement calmed down.

Shane felt disappointed; she never picked up the call and wondered if she had lost interest. Punching the keys once more, his phone rang. Hearing her voice on the other end, he sighed.

"Hi, there, I didn't even hear the phone ring as I was about to call you," he remarked.

"I'm in the library and couldn't talk while being in there. So, you actually called? I thought you might have forgotten about me. How have you been?"

"No, I hadn't forgotten about you at all, we have been busy," he replied, feeling elated.

"Greta, would you care to have lunch with me sometime? I know of a quaint place not far from my precinct where we could meet."

"Shane, I would love to meet up with you, yes that would be fun. Give me the address and we can set a date and time."

Greta was in her own world and feeling excited, began to skip as she continued to stroll along the walkway.

` ` `

James decided to take a drive downtown to clear his head, his plan was to visit Patrick's hangout later. The ladies of the night were out in full force.

As he pulled closer to the curb, he saw them all scattering; no one wanted to be arrested. As he got to closer to one of the ladies, he recognized Devine, "Hey there, have a minute to spear?"

She stopped and turned around to face him. A smile came across her face as she too recognized him.

"How are you Det.? I haven't seen you around here for some time now. What have you been up to, chasing the bad guys or the bad guys chasing you?" she asked.

"Hi Devine, I am doing ok, you have a minute?"

"Sure, what's up?"

"Can you get in the car so can we can speak more privately?"

"Any new information on Chili, I ask you about her before?"

"Ah yes, I do remember her, she still dances down by Elves. Oh, I did get an address for her if you want, it's on the other side of town, here it is, and I wrote it down."

"Thank you and here's something for your time," he said as he hands her some money.

```
` ` `
```

Now with an address for Chili, he had to decide whether he should first visit this location or go back to the homeless hang-out. He wondered if the information was accurate or he was being set up. He wasn't sure who to trust anymore.

Making a u-turn, he headed to the address provided to him and in a few minutes, came up on the house. Parking beyond the driveway, he walked back and quickly stepping through the gate. Climbing the stairs, he rang the bell.

Hearing footsteps walking towards the door, he stepped to the side and waited for it to be opened. Soon the big oak door slowly opened and standing there was one of the bouncers he recently put a beating on.

"You again, what the hell do you want this time? Are you a cop or what? Why are you harassing us?" asked Tom.

"Look, I only want to talk to Chili," said James.

"Well, if you aren't a cop, I won't give you shit and this time, you aren't going to get the better of me," Tom said as he stepped outside the door, closed it behind him and walked towards James.

"Look buddy, I'm not interested in you and your threats, I want to speak with Chili. She is the one I'm interested in, so save yourself the trouble, I'm not in the mood for your foolishness."

Lurching at him, Tom held him around his neck and tried to pull him down. James quickly raised his knees into his rib cage and watched him double over in pain. He followed the knee with a right hand across Tom's face and a left to his gut.

Coughing and gasping for air, he curled up into a ball to avoid any more punches. Searching him and finding no weapon, James stepped over him and walked into the house.

"Chili, oh Chili, I need to talk to you. I know you are here, come on out where ever you are."

From the corner of his eyes, he saw a shadowy figure lurking near a column and quickly turned around to face him. Charging at him was Ed with a baseball bat. Swinging it high above his head he landed the first blow in James' left palm. Wrestling it away, James swung it across his knees.

"You boys have not learnt anything from the last time. You need to find another line of work as this isn't one working out for you," said James as he began to climb the stairs.

Knocking on a closed door, he pushed it open and looked inside. Seeing no-one, he slammed it shut but not before dropping a vase on to the floor below. He walked back downstairs and stepping over Ed, exited the house.

Opening the closet door, Chili, crept into her bedroom, still shaking. She had never seen such brutality before especially by one person.

As he pulled away, James thought, "It was a waste of my time."

He was hoping she would contact Snake and he would now come to him rather than James searching for him.

` ` `

"Lucas, it's me, that man was here and he came inside looking for me. Yes, he beat up Tom and Ed again. Lucas, this guy is serious; he isn't afraid of anybody or anything. What are you going to do?"

"Chili, what do you mean, he was in your house, what kind of madman is he? Ok, I will deal with him, this can't go on." Lucas said while sinking deeper in his chair.

` ` `

Returning to the station, James asked Shane to pull up the locations of some of the business based on the information provided by Sarah. He knew if her name is on some, it was likely Snake would be tied to them too.

Soon, Shane provided him with the address of two other holdings and he selected one to visit it later. This time he would take Shane with him as he wanted him to learn as much as possible and furthermore for him to understand the underbelly of the city.

As darkness fell on the city, both James and Shane set out in an unmarked police utility vehicle; this night would be different. Slipping on their bullet-proof vests and checking their sidearm, they drove towards their target.

Pulling up two hundred yards from the intended target, both of them slipped on their masks and night goggles.

Peeping through the window, James saw several unidentified long boxes on the floor. Searching for any security alarm system and finding none, he slipped through a side door and crawled on his knees for a better look.

Opening one of the carts, it contained bales of cash wrapped in plastic bags packed to be shipped out. Waving at Shane to join him, both men began to remove the money and placed them in their duffle bags and walked out.

Turning around a corner, they spotted two men approaching them. Dropping their bags in the brushes next to them, they waited.

"What are you guys doing here at this time of the night? It s unusual for you to be taking a walk down here?" said one of the strangers.

"Look man, my buddy here and I were looking for a place to hang out, no worries, we will be on our way," said James.

"Not yet busters, we need to know why you are in this area," said the bigger of the two as he reach for James.

Reaching back, James punched him across the cheeks with all his might.

The other man grabbed Shane around the waist and tried to wrestle him to the ground. Shane hit him across the nose with his right elbow. As the man screamed in agony, he punched him on the side of his neck and watched him fall flat on his back.

With both men on the ground, they grabbed their bags and raced to their vehicle.

Down at the station, several officers counted the money brought in by both men. After two hours and six officers counting, the final total of the money was almost quarter million dollars.

Re-bagged and tagged, the money was placed in the evidence room. Sgt. Harris and the rest of the team congratulated both men on their victory but James deflected the honor to Shane.

"Shane did the hard lifting, not me."

He was about to object but James shut him down, "Enjoy it kid, you did well tonight, there will be other times for me."

Chapter 12

Lucas's veins bulged beneath his neck, "So, tell me something guys, I pay you to guard my money and you come here with this flimsy excuse. Two guys beat you up and stole it, what do you take me for? I can't trust Bini and now you are screwing me around."

Turning to look at the shorter of the two men, Tony, he continued, "And you, a one-time boxer don't even know to defend yourself? You are a poor excuse for a man,"

"No, Lucas, we are telling you the truth, these guys came out of nowhere and before we know it, they were on top of us," said Henry, defending Tony and himself.

"Why were you both outside the building when you know what we have in there?" Lucas asked as he hit Henry with a piece of led pipe.

"You, Henry, was suppose to be inside, not outside, and you Tony, how the hell you could make this person bust up your nose? Get out of my damn sight and find these two men or you will pay dearly," he said while raising the pipe once more.

Lifting up Henry, Tony quickly dragged him out of the way and they both sat in a corner of the room with bruised bodies and egos.

"Ah, boss, we believe those guys might have been cops, listen, think about it, it was dark yet they were able to see us long before we saw them. They knew what they were doing and they were both dressed in dark clothing, they had to be cops," said Tony.

"What's the name of this cop Bini been trying to get, William, is it? Is this the same guy who went to Chili's place and beat up Tom and Ed again? Well if it's him and he wants a war, I will give it to him; he is beginning to make me upset. Henry, you go and find out who is responsible for it and get an address for this man Williams. Don't come back here without an answer, whatever you do, don't give me the same bull shit Bini has been giving me, I won't stand of it."

With heads bowed, Tony and Henry quickly exited the room away from Lucas' steely stare; they knew he meant what he said.

"We need to speak with our guys on the street and see if they have heard anything," said Henry, still rubbing his bruised shoulder and face.

Tony said, "Let's go and speak with our women down on the street, they always know what's happening on the streets. First, let us go have a drink, Lucas has been hard on us and I need to think things through if we are going to get this policeman."

` ` `

Lucas was fidgety; he was the boss here but he also knew he was chicken-feed to those down in Central America. If he didn't deliver their cash, he knew there would be hell to pay and he needed to recoup the cash. He had to find a way to make up the money and the only way he could, was to have his ladies work harder and cut some corner with the quality of his drugs.

He now needed to get home; there was too much on his mind. Stepping through his front door, he heard Sarah talking on the phone. Keeping quiet, he crept behind and listened.

"My dear, listen, can we meet soon? There is so much we need to talk about and you know I can't do it from here, Lucas wouldn't allow it. I am so sorry our schedule did not allow us to meet up last week. Why not let us try for tomorrow at 2 pm. All right, we can meet at the cafe on 5th and 10th Street, bye."

He was still filled with rage and wanted to last out but decided not to. He would follow her to see who this person with whom she was speaking.

Tippy-toeing, he quietly walked back to the door, slowly opened and shut it with a bang before walking towards her.

Hearing loud slamming of the door, Sarah turned and walked into his arms and held him tight, "Hi honey, I didn't expect you home so soon. Can I get you anything?"

"No, I am good; I'm going to some rest before I go out later. Do you have any plans for tomorrow?" he asked.

"I had planned on seeing an old friend in the afternoon, why, do you have something you want us to do?"

"No, I'm only asking but would you like me to join you?"

Stuttering, she replied, "No need to, I know how busy you are and this is only a lunch date with an old friend."

Walking away from her, Lucas became more suspicious of her. He noticed how her face became rigid when he asked about joining her.

Henry and Tony were cruising downtown when they eventually saw one of their lackeys standing against a wall while smoking a cigarette.

Calling him over, Henry asked, "Have you heard anything on the streets about a recent robbery from a warehouse?"

"No man, there is no word on the streets. Where did it happen? I can ask around and see if I can hear anything and let you guys know. I have a friend who hustles along the streets near here. She might have some contact with the cops as she has never been arrested even though other women in her group have been," said his cohort.

Henry said, "Ok, that would be great, we will check with you tomorrow, so if you hear anything, we need to know, got me?"

` ` `

James' shift ended and he decided to hit a bar with some of the guys before he headed home; he had an hour or so to kill.

Walking into the "Skull" with Shane and two other officers, he quickly scanned the room.

Looking to his left, he thought he saw two guys who looked familiar.

Nudging Shane, he said, "Do those guys look familiar to you? I think they could be the same guys who tried to stop us the other night."

"You know what Det.? It sure looks like them."

James called out to the other officers, "Be on your guard, we may have some trouble."

From the corner of the room, Henry and Tony noticed the four men entering the bar and felt they appeared out of place; they were too well dressed and clean cut to be in a place like this.

Remembering the punch across his face and rubbing his cheek, Henry whispered, "Those guys look like the one who assaulted us. I need to check them out."

Walking to the bar and sitting next to James, Henry started a conversation with him, "Are you guys looking for a game of porker tonight?"

"Sorry, we are not, we are here to have a few beers and be on our way," replied James.

"I mean, nothing too big maybe a $20 a hand, you know, nothing fancy."

Turning to face him, James finally looked in his face. "What happened to your face mister?"

Before he could answer, Henry caught a glimpse of a gun handle under James' jacket and he swallowed hard. Now he knew for sure, this guy was a cop. Putting his drink to his head, he drank it all in one gulp.

Staring at his empty glass, Henry said, "I tripped over some boxes a few days ago and kind of knocked myself out." With a stiff smile and a wave of his empty glass, he said, "So sorry to have bothered you, have a good night," as he walked away.

James watched as he quickly headed to the back of the room and saw him whispering to his mate.

Shortly after, while looking over at James and his group, both men walked out of the bar.

Observing them, James nodded to Shane, "I will go out through the front while you two take the back door. Shane will follow me."

They were on no hurry to do so; they would be prepared for whatever the two strangers had in mind.

"I am telling you man, it's those two guys, they look like the ones who beat us up; it has to be them. I don't know the other two but the guy I was talking to have a gun under his coat. Guys like us hide our weapon but his is clearly on display, I need to pay him back," said Henry.

"If you are so sure don't you think we should call a few other guys to help us?" asked Tony.

"No Tony, you and me can handle this, we have dwelt with things like this before."

"Yes, but now we are talking about taking out cops, we can't afford to make any mistakes, and you remember what happened to Ed and Tom? I don't want to end up like them."

"What's this Tony, you turning chicken on me? Don't do this right now, we have a job to do and I tell you, those are the two guys. In case you forget, Lucas warned us about coming back without any answer," Tony said.

"I am not chickening out, I want to know we are correct, what if we are wrong? I don't want to kill an innocent cop," Tony said.

"Ok, Tony, make sure you back me up, when they come out, I will take out the big one and we high-tail it out of here."

Finishing his drink, James walked towards the door and slightly pushed it open. The moon reflected on the barrels of the guns the men held as they hid behind the shrubs.

Swinging the door wide open, James dropped to his knees and fired in their direction while rolling to left, away from the door. The flashes of rapid gun fire lit up the dark night.

Complete silence followed before James straightened up and moved towards the men. Shane and the others followed him. They found the men lying on the ground, still clutching their weapons; they were both lifeless.

Calling in the shooting, James and the others searched for the deceased identifications. He already believed they were working for Snake so it wouldn't be a surprise for him to know they are connected to him.

"What a night Det. Williams? There's always someone trying to get to you," said Shane

"Yes Shane, it happens sometimes but you and I know those guys were trying to pay us back for what we did to them. I guess we will be seeing more activity from Snake now that we have killed four of his men, arrested Sarah and taken his cash."

Lying in bed with Sarah by his side, Lucas was scanning the television stations when he saw a news alert.

"Two men were killed by the Police late this evening down at the Skull bar. They reportedly open fire on the officers who returned fire causing the two men to be fatally shot. At this time, we don't know their identities but once known, we will release the information, please stay tuned."

Reaching over her, he grabbed his cell and dialed Henry's number; it rang for sometime before someone answered.

"Henry?"

"Who is this?" The person on the other end of the line asked.

"Who the hell are you and why are you answering Henry's phone?"

"This is Det. Williams, now who are you, oh, could this be Lucas, the Snake? You should never send boys to do a man's job unless you are too chicken to do it yourself? Tell you what, come and get your boys and understand this, I will be coming for you next."

Turning to Shane, James said, "Guess what? Snake called his dead thug's phone, man he went off. It's just a matter of time before he will show his hands. All his boys are dropping like flies and his business is slowly drying up. Now all the pieces are falling into place. Let's wrap this up and get out of here, there is nothing more for us to do here tonight. Good job guys, I have to hand it to you, you were on the ball."

` ` `

His stomach in a knot, Lucas knew the cop was out to get him and dismantle his crooked empire. Flying into a rage, he kicked Sarah off the bed and began to curse at James and anyone else he could think of. Turning to face the mirror, he punched it and shattered the glass with splinters flying across the room, hitting both him and Sarah.

Screaming, Sarah shouted, "What the hell has come over you Lucas, why did you smash the mirror, look at what you caused and your hand? You are bleeding all over bed and the floor. Exactly who was on the phone and what happened?"

"This policeman Williams killed Henry and Tony. Now he is gloating over it and telling me he is coming for me. I am going to kill that bastard, I swear. He also took over half a million of my money. Tell me right now, were you seeing him, were you? If I find out you were, I promise you, I will take you out too. You of all the people should know I hate betrayal."

Sarah's chest tightened, she had never seen Lucas so angry and it scared her. She felt trapped and couldn't see any way out of the present situation.

She had the Police on her back and now Lucas threatening her. She was cornered and needed a way to get out of this dire. Could she try and convince James to listen to her and work with her to get rid of Lucas? She quietly walked into her bathroom and closing the door behind her, sat in a corner and began to sob; her world too, was slowly closing in.

She was concerned for her two daughters; what would happen to them if she were to be killed. They were not Lucas' children and while he had accepted them as part of the package, she knew they held no special place in his heart.

Often times, she caught him looking at them in a strange way; almost in a sexual manner but he had promised her, he would never trouble them in any way. She believed it would change quickly if she wasn't around.

She had no close relatives who would be willing to take on such a responsibility. The children's father had abandoned them; she was in a tight situation. For the next several hours, she sat in the corner, rocking back and forth in a state of shock.

Sunlight streamed through the bathroom window when the knock on the door startled her, "Who is it?" she asked.

"Mom, we couldn't help hearing the shouting last night and Lucas slamming the front door. Is everything ok?"

Opening the door, she pulled Sharon in, "Ah my dear, I am sorry you and your sister had to hear us. Lucas is having some problems with his business and he is frustrated, nothing else, so no need for you and your sister to worry."

"All right, mom, if you say so but look at your hand, there is blood all over it. Did he do this to you? Mom, you got to tell us if he is abusing you, we can get out of this, we don't need all this to be happy as long as we have each other."

"My child, it's a little more complicated than that, one day I will try and explain it all to you. Don't worry about it, I'm ok. Give me a few minutes to clean myself up, and we will talk later, love you both," she said while hugging her.

Sitting back on the floor, she felt ashamed, knowing her children were aware that things were not so right in her relationship. She knew she had to get away; if not for herself for their safety. Her chances now rest with James, no matter how he might feel about her. She also knew.

Chapter 13

James pulled into his driveway feeling wired and stressed from the events of the past evening. Inside, his family had already retired for the night and so he quietly moved through the house and headed for a quick shower.

Feeling refreshed, he crawled into bed and snuggled next to Bev. The warmth of her body excited him and he slowly reached for her as she turned around to face him.

Slumping in his arms, she sighed and held him tight, not wanting the moment to end, "Glad you came home at a decent time tonight, so nice to have you by my side", she said while running her fingertips across his chest.

Squirming, he said, "Stop or we will have another round."

Soon they both settled into a deep sleep.

` ` `

Late in the afternoon Shane and Greta finally meet for their first real date. Both appeared apprehensive and nervously laughed when they saw each other.

After a brief embrace and a kiss on her cheeks, Shane walked her into the restaurant and took a seat near the rear. Shane learned early in his job as a police man to always try and put his back to a solid wall whenever possible. Looking around, he scanned the area before looking at Greta and said,

"After chatting so much on the phone, it's nice to see you again. How have you been and what have you been up to?"

"Gosh, things have been interesting in the past few days, you know, me looking forward to the new school year and getting to know the area. I have a surprise to share with you too."

"What? Come on, do tell me, you can't keep me in suspense" he said while holding her hands across the table.

"Well, I am thinking of getting my own apartment."

"Wow, that's great but what made you decide to do. I thought you loved living at home?"

"Oh, I do enjoy living with them but it's time for me to be on my own, you know, find my own path in this crazy life."

"Well I am happy for you. When do you plan to make the move?"

"I have been looking and my mom has volunteered to help me with the search. I am hoping to find something soon, you know, before school starts."

"Fantastic; do you want me to help you? I am from around here so I could take you around whenever you want to look at something."

"I would like that if I wouldn't be taking up too much of your time."

"Nah, It would be my pleasure to help you."

The attendant waltzed over to take their order and the both of them laughed as they realized they had yet to look at the menu.

"Two love-birds, I will give you a few more minutes" said the attendant with a smile as she walked away.

At the end of the meal, Shane walked her to her car and for the first time, kissed her on the lips as she pulled him close.

Getting in her car, she asked, "Would you mind if my mom came along with us to look at the apartments? I don't want to impose my family on you if you are not comfortable with it."

Smiling, he said, "It will be fine with me if she wants to come along."

Greta could not believe how well they both related to each other and found fun in simple thing like having a meal together. She definitely was hoping he would be considering what it would mean to them both if she were to find her own place.

Shane felt excited after seeing her and the prospect of her getting her own place intrigued him. He noted she had made no reference of him and her when speaking about finding her own place. The thought of staying there greatly intrigued him.

He realized he had never thought about living on his own; he was comfortable living with his parents. He also felt a little guilty should he leave them seeing they had invested so much in his education. He felt he needed to pay them back and leaving would not be the best thing. Putting aside those thoughts, he got in his car and turning in the opposite direction to her, headed out on his way.

` ` `

Sarah got up mid-morning with plans to meet her mystery person and Lucas pretended to be asleep while she got ready. He watches she took care and time to dress, she looked sexy in her short skirt and blouse exposing her midriff.

He was conflicted in regards to his feelings towards her, the night before, he felt he wanted to make love to her but in his mind, he felt uneasy about her coming and goings. As such even if she was interested in being intimate with him, his emotions were of such he would not have been a good lover.

Looking back at Lucas lying in the bed, Sarah felt sorry for him; he provided well for her and her children but beyond that, he wasn't the person she wanted to spend her life with. The one person she wanted, she couldn't have for several reasons namely he was married and secondly, they both were on opposite sides of the law.

She still hoped to one day get out of Lucas' control but still she wanted to enjoy the quality of life she experienced before being arrested. Again she thought if she was to help James take him down, the court would give her a reduced sentence. She wanted to try once again if only James would give her a chance.

She knew she had nothing to lose, now caught between a rock and hard place. She decided she would call James once again.

Seated at the breakfast table with his family, James said, "Well Dudley, your mom and I talked about your coming home on your own after school. We agreed you can do it if you want to, however, there will be certain guidelines. What do you say?"

With his two siblings giggling, he said, "I would like that, dad."

"Ok, here is what your dad and I are going to do, we will give you a cell phone, but you will only be allowed to call me, you dad or home, no games on it as you have your tablet. You must be home no later than an hour after school ends and you must call one of us to let us know you are home. We aren't trying to monitor your movements but we need to know you are not in any trouble. Do you think you can follow those rules?" Bev asked.

Both Sharon and John said in unison, "What about me mom?"

"When you both get a little older, we will talk about it. Right now, we are talking about Dudley," Bev replied.

"Yes mom and dad, I promise to follow the rules, thanks."

"Great, now that's settled, you kids clean up and get ready for school. Dudley, we will start next Monday, ok." James said.

``` ` ` ` ```

Driving beneath the mid-day sun, Sarah's mind was cloudy with many thoughts; she would meet this friend and take it from there.

Two blocks away behind her, Lucas was following. He had no reason to rush as he already knew exactly where she was going and what time she would meet this "friend."

Pulling into the parking lot of the restaurant, Sarah parked and sat in the car for a few minutes checking her make-up

A tap on the trunk of her car startled her, and turning around, she saw an old flame, Matt. She had not seen him for the past several years and didn't even know he was in her area. Getting out, she greeted him with a kiss on the cheeks and a warm embrace.

"Hello Matt, I haven't seen you in a long time since you left us. How are you doing?"
```

"Hi Sarah, it's been a long time, and a lot of things have happened since we broke up but I'm doing alright now. Look at you, you sure look fine. What are you doing on this part of town?

"I am meeting a friend for lunch. Would you like to join us?"

"Thank you that would be lovely."

From afar, Lucas observed the interaction especially what looked to him like an intimate kiss. Fuming, he laid into his car horn and screamed while other drivers stared at him.

Getting a hold of himself, he drove past where Sarah had parked and as he passed her car, she was still embracing this strange man. Finding a parking lot a short distance away, he walked the short distance to where she was, always looking around behind him.

Sarah and Matt began to walk towards the restaurant when she heard her name being called.

"Sarah, wait up for me."

Looking around, she saw her friend waving wildly at her and stopping, she waited.

"Well hello Pearl, you made it on time. You remember Matt? We ran into each other after all these years. Matt, you remember Pearl don't you?"

"Hi Pearl, yes, of course, how could I forget you, nice seeing you again. I guess you ladies were going to hang out for awhile, I should leave you alone."

"No need to leave, we can catch up on old times, it's been a long time since we both saw you," said Pearl as they selected a table close to the exit.

Sitting down, they all soon became engrossed in a conversation.

Appearing in front of them was Lucas and Sarah recoiled in her seat.

"Lucas, what are you doing here, I thought I left you at home in bed, were you following me? This is Matt and you know Pearl.

"Ladies, I best be going, it was nice to see you and Pearl again after all these years," said Matt.

"Matt, is it? You sit the hell down. I need to know what's going here. First, I hear you making plans to meet someone and now I see you with this guy and Pearl. Are you in on this too Pearl?"

"Listen Lucas, I'm not sure exactly you are talking about. Sarah and I planned to meet up today and I guess Matt happened to be in the area. I know this, so you can tell us if you know something else," Pearl replied.

"Lucas, please listen to Pearl, it's the truth, she and I planned to meet here and Matt happened to see us. Anyway, you have not answered me, why the hell were you following me and why did you feel the need to listen in on my conversation?

"I don't know anymore Sarah, I heard you on the phone and became suspicious and now seeing you with this guy, make me crazy. I have never heard you speak of Matt before."

"Look, Matt has been a friend for many years, long before you and I got together but we are only friends. You need to get a hold of yourself; lately you get quite upset easily and for the least little thing, I am not sure what's going on with you."

"Sarah, watch your mouth. Who are you to tell me I have been acting strange, you forgot who you are talking to?"

"You know what Pearl and Matt? Let's get the hell out of here. He wants to create a scene and I am not prepared to deal with this crap right now," Sarah said.

Rising up from the chair, Sarah turned to walk away when he reached across the table and with an open hand, slapped her across the face, knocking her back into the chair.

"You want to walk out on me; you think I will let you go? There is no way you are going to do this to me," he said as he raised his right hand once more.

Reaching over the table, Matt punched him in the face, knocking him down to the ground. While lying on the ground, Lucas reached under his coat but Matt was on top of him in a split second, punching him several times.

The women screaming caused Matt to stop the assault. Standing over Lucas, he looked at the frightened women staring at him. He also noticed others were watching.

"Get out of here ladies, I am sure the cops will be here soon, no need for you to stick around. I will make sure he doesn't follow you," Matt said while taking a seat next to where Lucas remained laying on the ground.

Lucas in a daze, no one had ever punched him out before and here he was, on the ground and the assailant had not run away.

Watching him on the ground, Matt said, "Lucas my boy, you got to stop beating up on your women, one of these days, you are going to get yourself killed by one of them. If you want to take out your frustration on someone, take it out on a man like yourself. I thought you were a bigger man than those who beat up on their women, shame on you."

Matt stood up and simply walked away; never looking back. He knew Lucas would not dare to do anything seeing other the customers had seen what had happened.

Slowly getting up off the ground, Lucas brushed himself off and looked around; Matt and the women were nowhere to be seen. Hearing the Police siren getting closer, he hurried out; he would get his revenge later.

When the Police arrived, they found no witness the bartender who provided some information.

` ` `

"Sarah, what are you going to do now? You can't go back home right now. Lucas will certainly be mad at you especially seeing Matt punched him out. He must think you put him up to it," says Pearl.

'I am not sure but I will figure something out. I don't want to think about it right now. Let's try and enjoy this time together as we don't get to do this too often."

"Ok Sarah, but are you sure he won't follow us again? He scared the hell out of me when he appeared in front of us."

"Thank God you were there, can you imagine if he had come there and saw only Matt and myself, I think he would have completely lost it. Actually, I was happy Matt was there. Did you notice how quickly he reacted and punched Lucas? Never saw someone move so quickly," Sarah said.

"Tell you what, why don't you come and stay with me for a few days, at least until he calms down? We can get the kids later today and my place is big enough for you all to stay for awhile if you want. No one will bother you."

"Thanks Pearl, it sounds great; we can hang out for a few days. I know he will get over it soon, and will be calling around if he doesn't see me in a few days."

` ` `

James looked at his cell phone and saw there was another message from Sarah and thought; she certainly would not give up. He had no interest in contacting her; he had Snake on the offense and knew it was a matter to time before he showed his hands. Snake had now lost four of his men and lots of money; he would be feeling desperate, and desperate men do foolish things.

He would also hold out Sarah for as long as he felt it necessary; she too was desperate based on the number of times she tried to reach him. He would make a quick stop and collect an item from the pharmacy.

Behind the counter the pharmacist, Josephine was busily filling out prescriptions; she a mere five feet, two inches tall. She appeared to be a happy person as she was always smiling. She greeted James and quickly handed him his pre-ordered item.

Acknowledging her smile and thanking her for the quick service, he was in and out in a short time.

Standing outside of the building, he felt the sun bearing down on him. Walking to his car, he started it, and turned on the air conditioner. The cool air felt good on his skin so he sat there for a few minutes. From the corner of his eyes, he thought he saw someone familiar and turning around saw Sarah and an unidentified woman briskly walking along the street.

Getting out, he decided to follow them from a safe distance. He wondered if this person next to Sarah was Chili but figured it couldn't have been her based on her size

At the ice-cream stand, Sarah and Pearl were busy trying to decide what kind of ice cream to select; they didn't see when the stranger walked in and stood behind them.

"Hello Sarah," said James.

Her heart almost stopped when she heard the voice; she would recognize his voice anywhere and turning around, she came face to face with James.

Before she could say a word, Pearl said, "Is this going to be another scene like Lucas and Matt?"

"No I don't think so, this is Det. Williams, the guy I told you about you, you know, the guy. Johnny, this is my friend, Pearl."   "Oh, yes, nice to meet you Det. fancy us seeing you here," said Pearl.

"Hi Pearl, nice to meet you, I was getting something from the pharmacy when I noticed Sarah and you walking by. So, Sarah, I see you are enjoying a day out. What exactly happened to you? Pearl said something about an incident involving Lucas."

"Nothing, it's no big deal. I left you several messages and you never responded to any and now here you are."

"Well, I guess I have been busy, you know the deal. Anyway, I saw you and wanted to say hello, I'll be on my way. Pearl, again, nice meeting you, see you around."

"Johnny, please wait up, what if I give the information you want on Lucas, would you reconsider us?"

"I am not sure what you could give me as we have been down that road too many times before, and we both know how they all ended.,

"Look, meet me in the library tomorrow around 2 pm and I will provide you with the information. The library is a safe place for us to meet, right? I promise, I will tell you everything."

"Now why would you want to do that, I thought Snake was your partner, why the sudden change of heart?"

"Meet me and I'll tell you all about it. Maybe you will understand I am being sincere."

"Ok, Sarah, I'll meet you but know this, I will not be there alone so if you have other plans, be prepared for the worse."

Sarah tried to hold him but he kept on walking and with tears in her eyes, she returned to join her friend, no longer interested in ice cream.

Chapter 14

Bini couldn't make any contact with Sarah; all his messages went to her voice-mail and she wasn't returning his calls. She promised to work with him one more time and not hearing from her, he was worried. Any further failure would be the end of him; he and Sarah had to get their act together. He decided he too had nothing to lose and so he planned to visit Lucas house once more.

As darkness fell, time came for him to get some answers and so he headed to the secluded home. Coming half a mile away from the house, he stopped and sat there for a few minutes trying to calm his nerves. Dressed in black; he needed to get in and out as quickly as possible.

Along the high wall, he crept, this time he wouldn't dare go through the front gate. Up against the house, he slowly checked each window. Hearing voices, he looked into the great room and saw Lucas on the phone, screaming at someone.

"You got to get rid of this guy Matt; he got in my face the other day and embarrassed me in front of Sarah and her friend. I don't give a damn how you do it and while you are at it, get rid of Bini too. He is no longer useful to me; he has been a complete failure. What? No, I will deal with Sarah myself, whatever you do, don't go near her."

Quickly turning around, Lucas called out, "Is someone there?"

Ducking beneath the window, Bini began to retreat as the flood-lights came on and temporarily blinded him.

Out of breath, he headed for the fence but never made it. Behind him, he heard the dogs running after him and they were right behind him. Turning around and with his gun drawn, he fired as rapidly as he could. He never made it to the fence.

Calling off the dogs, Lucas' men found what was left of Bini; he had been torn to bits.

Police officers were dispatched to the residence and while the officers spoke with the men, Lucas hid inside. From his bedroom window, he watched as they walked around his yard.

One of the officers who visited the residence was Shane and he recalled hearing the address before.

Strolling to the man giving his statement, Shane asked, "Who owns this residence?"

Looking down at the ground, the man remained silent.

"Sir, we do need to know who the owner is so we can verify all this information, you do need to answer."

Without looking directly at the policeman, the man replied, "He is not available, he is out of the country and we are watching it for him."

"Sir, I didn't ask you where he was, I asked you, what his name is. This much you can tell me or is there something you are hiding from us?"

"No officer, he wouldn't like to know someone died on his property while he was away and giving his name with him not being present is not such a good idea."

"For the last time, what is his name? And don't tell me you don't know or I will charge you with obstruction. Maybe you are the owner and you actually released the dogs on the deceased," said Shane.

"No, no, it's not my house and I never released the dogs on the guy. Ok, ok, his name is Parrish."

"That wasn't so hard. What's your name and do you have any identification?" asked Shane.

After confirming the man's ID, he moved on to speak with the coroner and once the body was released, Shane began to look around the outside of the house.

It was a large house situated on quite a big property in an affluent neighborhood. Nothing looked out of place; things appeared to have been placed exactly where they should be; almost too perfect.

` ` `

At the station, James was coming out of the bathroom when Shane walked in and sat down at his desk, "Had a busy night Shane?"

"Det. Williams, you would never will believe what happened, while you were out, we got a call about a dog attack on some poor soul and guess where it happened?"

He saw the excitement on Shane's face and waited.

"It happened at one of the address we checked belonging to Sarah but the guys there said it belonged to one Parrish."

"Is that right? Well that's interesting, I also had an interesting conversation with Sarah earlier today. She wants to tell me all about him tomorrow."

"So are you going to meet with her?"

"Yes Shane, you and I will meet her and see how much truth there is to her story. Finish up your report and let's meet back here tomorrow around mid-day to meet Ms. Sarah Brown."

` ` `

Lucas felt the winds of failure passing through him; he did not feel sorry about Bini but it had brought the cops to his house.

Standing in his great big house, Lucas felt alone. If anyone were to have asked him if he missed her, he would say not for a minute, he didn't care. Deep down, it was a different story.

He knew was she strong-willed and would do whatever she wanted. There was little he could do to change her mind. Past experience also told him she would fight back. He had to find a way to get to her and hopefully she would understand and eventually come back home.

Sarah was lounging around Pearl's pool when she heard the news. When the announcer read the address, she dropped the drink and as it crashed onto the pool deck. Rushing inside the house, she dialed a number.

"Lucas, what the hell happened there last night, who was it?"

"Ah, you finally decide to call. Where are you and when are you coming home?"

"Lucas, I need to know what's happening. You think I would run back to you after you slapped me in public. You know better now, tell me what happened last night."

"It was Bini, not sure what he was doing outside the house again but the dogs attacked him."

"Oh my lord, Bini is dead?"

"He had it coming anyway; he caused me too many losses even in death as now the cops came here. I can't afford to have them coming here. Sarah, are you coming home, I want you to come back and am sorry for assaulting you."

"What about Matt, are you going to try and hurt him too? You know he was only defending me."

"No Sarah, I have no interest in him, it's in the past."

"I will have to think about it, I will call you in a couple of days and let you know."

"Ok, but listen Sarah, I won't wait too long for you to give me an answer. If I don't hear from you within the next few days, you and your children can do whatever you want, but you won't be coming back here."

"Lucas, you know how I feel about ultimatums, I don't give a shit and I will call you when I am ready. Whatever you do, don't forget it's me, the one who sleeps in your bed with you at nights."

"Look, it's not a threat, I am tired of asking you about things, you seem aloof these days, and seeing you with that guy pushed me over the edge. Alright, take your time and let me know when you decide."

Numbness in her brain caused her to slump in the chair, while she and her children felt safe with Pearl, it wasn't their place. She also knew things wouldn't be the same between Lucas and her.

Getting up, she hurried inside and began to dress for her meeting with James. Her thoughts rested on Bini; she never really cared for him but they shared a lot over the years. Now she was feeling guilty for not having responded to any of his texts or calls.

Listening to Lucas, he still sounded angry and she did not like how he paused before answering when she asked him about Matt. She knew he never forgets anything, especially another man whopping his ass and not running away.

` ` `

Matt carefully walked on both sides of the law; he owned a respectable company in the adjoining city but was above dipping his hands into something illegal for quick cash. He once was a professional boxer, kept himself in good physical shape and a pair of fists like clubs.

Driving from Pearl's home, Sarah was thinking of Bini, Matt, James and even Lucas. She wondered if she would be doing the right thing by selling Lucas out to James, "What if after all, James wanted nothing to do with me? What if Lucas was to get killed, would Matt be still interested in me?" she thought.

Coming into the intersection, she didn't see the stop sign and sped right through.

The screeching brakes and sudden impact of her vehicle being smashed shook her out of the trance. Looking around, she saw the truck partially on its side with the trailer lying in the ditch. Staggering out of her car, she slowly approached the truck; not sure what to expect.

Slowly opening his door, the driver walked over to her, "Why the hell didn't you look where you were going? You have destroyed my truck and now I have lost my load. Call the cops and show me your insurance papers," the man said.

"I am so sorry, but look at my car, how am I going to get to where I'm going?"

"Lady, I don't care about your damn car, this is your entire fault. Who is going to pay me for my truck?"

"Listen sir, I am sorry but you and I know the insurance companies will take care of this so cool it, it was an accident."

Having exchanged their insurance information, both the other driver and Sarah waited for the Police and paramedics to arrive. She didn't feel she needed them but then felt a warm liquid on her face and wiped it away. With blood on her hands, she began to freak out and lay on the ground. The paramedics soon arrived and while treating her, they noticed the bracelet strapped to her leg. Calling the Police over, they showed them the monitor and it didn't take them long to figure who she was.

Seeing she had serious contusions, she was taken to the hospital while the truck driver was examined and released. The officers radioed the station; their intention to travel with the injured female to the local hospital.

` ` `

James, who was still at the station, listened in on the call and when they called her name, he decided to pay a visit to the hospital.

Arriving in the hospital, James saw Candy and her eyes lit up as she walked out and greeted him.

"Sarah Brown was admitted here. Which room is she located?" he asked.

Pointing to the room, Candy noticed how he paused before entering the room.

"Do you know her, Jay?"

"Why do you ask?" he asked.

"When she came in, she was mumbling and asking for you so I figure you must know her. Well, do you?" Candy asked.

"Actually, yes, I do know her, Candy. I am the reason why she is wearing a bracelet on her ankle."

"Wow, you must tell me about it someday. I will see you when you are through."

Watching as she walked away, he noticed how pronounced her walk was and he chuckled. Staring at Sarah, she opened one eye and looked at him.

"You came to look for me baby? So nice to see you, I was coming to see you when this happened."

Pulling up a chair next to her, he asked, "What exactly happened to you?"

As she spoke, he noticed Candy passing by the room a few times and while she looked in, she never entered.

The truck driver was still at the accident site. Finding his phone, he called his boss, "Mr. Ruff, unfortunately I had an accident, no sir, I wasn't at fault. A woman drove through the intersection into the side of the truck. I am sorry sir, could you have one of the guys come by and get the contents? Here is the intersection where I'm at."

"What about you and the other driver were either of you hurt and you did say it was a woman?" Matt asked.

"I will be ok, a bit shaken up and yes sir; she was taken to the hospital with possible broken bones. Once the Police came, they wouldn't allow me to speak with her but I did get her name."

"What is her name? I could go and visit her and find out if she going to be ok," Matt replied.

"Just a minute, her name is Sarah Brown."

"Did you say Sarah Brown?" asked Matt.

"Yes sir, are you ok, do you know her?"

"Yes, I do know her. Alright, no worries, I'll take care of it."

Reclining behind his desk, Matt smiled and thought, "What are the chances of such series of events happening to me in such a short time."

He would pay her a visit if nothing more than to reassure her he would take care of the accident.

"May I have a few words with you?" Candy asked.

Looking around, he noticed Candy standing by the door with her hands on her hips as to say she was getting impatient.

Sarah also noticed this and looking at James asked, "Why is she so demanding of you. Is there something going on between you two?"

"Sarah, right now, you are not in any position to ask such a question. I am here to get some information about Snake, seeing you won't be meeting me at the library."

Turning to Candy once more, he said, "I will be with you soon, am speaking with Miss Brown."

Returning his attention to Sarah, he asked, "So are you going to tell me what I need to know about Snake?"

"Johnny, what will you do with the information if I tell you? I can't afford for it to get out. Lucas would certainly kill me."

"Sarah, this is not the time to play games, either you are going to talk to me or I am out of here for good. I am tired of your games. Once I walk out that door, that's it, you won't see me again until the time of the trial and it will be too late for me to help you."

Grimacing, she sat up and began to lay out what she knew about Lucas and all his associates.

James was finally getting the full picture of Snake's operations and all his sources. Now he had to dismantle his businesses and the cartel would take care of the rest. While he would have loved to have personally taken him out, he knew he had sworn to protect life and only take it when absolutely necessary.

Sarah then asked, "Will I be safe after all this? What will happen at the trial? I can't afford to do any time as Lucas will be able to have his men get to me in there."

"I will speak with the Crown Attorney on your behalf and see if she will consider some leniency based on the information you have provided. I can't make any promises as to what she will do but if we do get Snake, we will see. I will have two officers stand outside of your room tonight."

Handing him a picture, she said, "Ok, Johnny, I would appreciate any help you can give me. By the way, here is a picture of Lucas as I am not certain you know what he looks like. Sometimes he wears a toupee and changes his appearance."

"Thanks, I would never have known this is how he looks."

Turning to leave, James came face to face with another man standing in the doorway. With his hand on his gun, he turned to her and asked, "Who is this?"

"Hi, I am Matt, a friend of Sarah, and you are?"

"Ah, you are the person I heard Sarah and her friend talk about, nice to meet you, I am Det. Williams. I will leave you two to talk."

"Sarah, I will be in touch."

"That would be nice, thank you."

Pulling up a chair next to Sarah, Matt said, "What was that all about? I got your message and next thing one of my drivers called to say you had an accident with him."

"That was your driver? I am so sorry. I have so much going on, I must have missed the sign," she said.

"No worries, it has been taken care of, I came down here to see how you are doing. Did I hear you tell the officer Lucas has threatened to kill you, why?"

"Oh Matt, it's a long story and I am not sure you want to get involved in my mess. I have to find my way out of it, you see this?" as she shifted the covers from her leg and showed him her ankle bracelet. "This is all because of Lucas and his business affairs."

"Jesus, Sarah, what the hell did you do?"

"You remember a few months ago two men were killed in a park by the Police? Yes, I was in the middle of it so here I am."

"I am so sorry, how can I help and please don't say I can't. I have the resources."

"Oh Matt, I can't even think straight right now, I want Lucas to be out of my life for good. The kids are not happy with the situation right now."

"What do you mean, he is threatening our kids. I need to know as it's one thing I will not stand for."

"No Matt, he has not done anything but they heard us arguing a few nights and they were crying; it broke my heart."

"Why don't you let them come and live with me while we sort out this situation, you know I can take care of them."

"Right now they are staying with Pearl; let them stay there for now until things settle down."

"Alright, we will see this through and take it from there. So, any broken bones, how are you feeling now? Do you think they are going to keep you overnight?"

"I am not sure but you can ask the nurse. They are waiting for the doctor to come by."

"Ok, we will wait; in the meantime, I will stay here with you."

"Thanks Matt, it's good to have you here."

Chapter 15

Strolling to the nurses' desk, James saw Candy's smile changed to a frown and it puzzled him, "Is everything ok, you looked upset with my speaking with Ms. Brown. Is there something I am not aware of?"

"Nothing is wrong, sorry if my emotions show on my face. I thought she was a bit too personal with you. I must have been mistaken, sorry," she replied with a feigned smile on her face.

"Now Candy, am I sensing you are jealous? Rests assure my business with her is strictly professional. Now where were we, what you say we go and get a cup of coffee downstairs?"

"Sorry, I can't leave my post right now, not until someone comes to relieve me but why don't you give me a call later? I get off around three this evening but have a few errands to run until around seven or so."

"Ok, I can do that and you are sure you're alright?"

"No, I'm fine. By the way, who is the guy with her now?" as she pointed towards Sarah's room.

"I have no idea; I met him when he walked into the room. Why do you ask?"

"Oh nothing, I have seen him here before but can't put my fingers on when it. Oh well, they know each other quite well, see how he is holding her hands? He's no stranger," Candy replied.

James kept telling himself he didn't care one way or the other but deep down he was feeling left out. H wasn't going to let Candy know especially now she invited him to her house.

"All right, I will give you a call sometime after ten. By the way, make a copy of this picture and keep it on file. If your staff sees this person, do not let him go near Ms. Brown's room and notify the policemen at her door," James said.

"She must be important for you to have police guard her room."

"Yes she is vital to the case I am working on."

` ` `

At the accident, a driver assisting thought he knew the car involved and on closer inspection, confirmed it. "Where is the driver of this car?" he asked.

"She was transported to the hospital," a Policeman replied.

Calling his boss, he said, "I am here at an accident and guess whose car was involved?"

"Jason, I am not in the mood to play any guessing game, tell me whose it is."

"It's Sarah's car and she has been taken to the hospital

"Thanks, you make sure you take it to my dealer; don't let anyone else move it."

Lucas was excited yet worried all at the same time. He now knew where Sarah was yet concerned for her safety. He still cared about her no matter what he told her or anyone else and decided to visit her at the hospital later.

As the sun set high in the sky, Lucas pulled out of his driveway and paused for a moment at the red paint on the ground. Along the way, reminiscing about his life, he thought of all the lives he has taken or caused to be taken. He told everyone, he didn't have a choice, and the life chose him instead.

Arriving at the hospital and not spotting a police vehicle, he walked towards the nurses' desk and asked, "Is there a patient named Sarah Brown here?"

The nurse in charge said to him, "Kindly wait a moment while I check the list for patient's room," while she pressed the alarm and notify the Police guarding Sarah's room.

From the corner of his eyes, Lucas saw an officer walking towards him and the look at the nurse told him what had occurred.

As he was retreating, one of the Policemen called out to him by his name, "Lucas Wise, stop there, we need to speak with you."

Glancing behind him, he saw the officer approaching with his weapon drawn. Skipping the stairs, two at a time, Lucas's feet were moving like a locomotive. Eventually finding a large garbage bin at the corner of the building and his heart pounding, hid behind it, "Did Sarah set me up and the Police knew I would try and see her?" he thought.

One thing he knew for sure, the Police and hospital workers now knew what he looked like. He was certain Sarah had given him up otherwise they wouldn't have known him.

Waiting for several minutes and no longer hearing footsteps, he quickly walked to his car, parked some distance away. Safely back inside, he swore at Sarah and everyone else. He felt Sarah had to be eliminated; she had too much on him. He remained at his location for several minutes, pondering his next move.

In the hospital room, the Policeman spoke with Sarah and Matt. Holding her hands, Matt said, "I will run out for a few minutes to get fresh set of clothes, l will be back shortly. I will also make sure you are ok."

Biting her lips, she held him tight, "Don't be too long."

` ` `

Still fuming, Lucas saw a lone figure making his way across the hospital parking. Looking closer, he thought he looked familiar so he slowly pulled away and began to drive towards the person. A short distance away, he realized who it was Matt and he sped up towards him.

Hearing the approaching car, Matt noticed it was coming right at him. Jumping out of the way, he pulled his gun and fired three quick rounds at the driver's window. The window shattered as the driver continued to drive away. He didn't get a good look at the driver but thought it might have been Lucas.

Looking around he saw no one and picking up the casings, he returned to the hospital. Stepping into Sarah's room, he stood by the entrance for a few seconds to watch her.

Sarah eyes opened wide, seeing him standing there with what looked like torn clothes.

"Gosh, you returned already, what happened to your clothes?" she asked.

"It's funny you should ask. I was in the parking lot when someone drove at me. What car does Lucas usually drive?"

"He usually drives a bimmer, but why?"

"Well, he is the one who drove at me but I shot at him before he fled."

"I am so sorry Matt, I keep drawing you into my problems, and I can't believe he would be such a fool. I guess he is getting desperate."

"Listen, don't worry about it, by coming after me, he is now making it my war. He will be sorry he tried, and I have a feeling he was wounded I shot right at his window. If he is, he won't be able to come back here."

"Oh Matt, I hope you got him and he will be out of my life for good. I think he is a bit crazy."

"I will freshen up in your bathroom and stay here; I can manage with these clothes for now. I'll have one of my boys bring me some fresh clothes later."

Lucas was driving so fast out of the parking lot; he jumped the curb and almost collided with the fence. He felt something warm on his left arm, but couldn't afford to look at it; he needed to get the vehicle under control.

Half a kilometer down the road, he finally slowed down and pulled off the road and began to inspect himself. Pulling up his shirt, he saw he was shot in the shoulder but felt it in the lower arm. Glass splinters scattered in the cabin.

Cursing, he pulled off his belt and tied it above the wound. Exiting the vehicle, he brushed off the broken glass and called an acquaintance to meet him at the house with his medical bag; there was urgency in his voice. The Police were notified of gun-fire and officers rushed over there. Searching the lot, they didn't find any evidence of gunplay.

Reviewing the CTV images, they realized there was an altercation in the parking lot. They were unable identify the parties and no gun-shot victim reported to the hospital. James had a few hours to spare before he calls Candy so he took a drive near Snake's construction company's office.

Pulling into the yard, the place looked deserted with machinery laying about the place; none appeared to be in working order. The place looked like a front for illegal business. James would have loved to speak to someone; anyone who could provide information on Snake.

It was after 10 PM when James called Candy from the Police station, "What are you up to right now?"

"I'm waiting for your call. Can you get away for a bit and come by?"

"Sure, I could stop by in a few minutes if it's ok with you," he said.

"I ask if you wanted to come by so yes, it's ok with me, here is the address."

"Ok, I will be there soon. I have to complete a report here on my desk."

Sinking in his chair, he wondered if he should follow through with meeting her. Putting down the telephone, Bev's words and his friend Jack coming back to him. He felt he was still in control and could stop whenever he wanted but right now, he wasn't ready.

As he pulled into the driveway, the garage door opening and assumed it was for him. Once inside, the door closed and an inner door left ajar.

Stepping inside the house, he saw her standing in front of him, dressed in a baby-blue teddy. In her hands were two glasses of drinks and she handed one to him.

Politely taking the glass from her, James placed it on a side table and they sat down on the sofa with Candy keenly watching him as she sipped her drink. Chuckling and reaching past him, she took his glass and drank from it.

"My, you are a cautious person. You tend not to trust people but it's ok, I like that," she said.

"Sorry, it's a habit," he said while now reaching for his drink.

"So, Jay, do you like what you see?"

Nodding his head, he smiled; her nurse's outfit did not do her any justice. She was voluptuous with a well defined backside with a relatively small waist. Standing in front of him, she looked beautiful.

Before he could answer, she began to slowly strip; not that she had many to take off, it was only two pieces. Soon she stood completely naked in front of him and waiting for his response.

Putting down his drink, he scooped her up in his arms and asked, "Where is the bedroom?"

Hugging him tightly around his neck and with a wide grin, she pointed and said, "It is right behind you."

Walking towards it, he gently laid her down on the bed and quickly stripping off his clothes, he soon joined her beneath the covers and became lost in her arms.

Candy was the first to speak, "Well, it was certainly worth the wait, now I know why I'm so attracted to you; it's your animal instinct. We will have to do this again."

"Ah, you were amazing, we will see how things go as I do have a family as I have already mentioned," James said.

"Oh, I know, I promise you, no pressure at all. As you can see, this is my house and I live alone so no worries."

"As much as it would be nice to stay longer with you, I must head back to the station as I am still on the job."

"I understand, the bathroom is over there, and you can freshen up before you leave. Will I see you at the hospital soon?"

"As long as the patient is there I will come by, but, I now know your home address so we will see."

` ` `

Lucas was lying on his big bed alone with his arm now in a cast. His friend was there when he got home and quickly patched up the wound.

After extracting the bullet, he stitched up the hole and placed a bandage around the area, 'Now, you need to rest that arm.'.

Lucas replied, "Fine, now, I expect this will remain between you and me. If words get out about this, I could have some trouble and I am not prepared for that, you understand?"

While tucking away the wad of cash given to him, the friend said, "I have no reason to mention this to anyone; your information has always been safe with me."

He was also thinking Matt was more of a trouble maker than he first thought; punching him out was one thing but now he actually shot him. He now knew he was no match for Matt and he and his gang would have to surprise him if they were going to take him down.

` ` `

While at the station, James was informed of Snake's attempt to visit Sarah and a possible shooting in the parking lot and he made him wonder if both were related. Calling Shane, he said, "Let's go the hospital, there's a new development."

Along the way, the topic of Greta came up and James asked, "How things were going with you both?"

"Well, we finally had a dinner date and I actually met her mother."

"Wow, you are certainly moving fast. Are you sure that was   such a good idea to meet her mother so soon?"

"It's nothing like that, she was looking for an apartment and I agreed to take her around and her mother came along."

"And did she quiz you non-stop?"

"Not all, Greta introduced me as a friend and her mother appeared to be quite nice and we got along ok," Shane replied.

"So, does this mean you are going to move in with her once she finds something?"

"Actually she found a nice apartment near her school but no, I don't think so, she never mentioned it. Furthermore, I want to give back my parents some money that they spent on me while I attending college. If she asks me I guess I will have to think about it but right now, it's not on my radar."

"Well buddy, believe me, it's going to be sooner than you think, you can bet on," said James.

Shane chuckled and said, "You think so? I guess we will see and don't laugh, I will tell you if it happens. So why are we heading back to the hospital, did something happen to Ms. Brown?"

"Nah, I heard Snake might have tried to see her and there shooting even though no bullets were found. I have a suspicion they might be related," replied James.

"Oh? Is Snake hooked on her or is he trying to harm her?"

James said, "She knows too much about him and from what she told me, he wants to kill her so maybe that's why he came by earlier. Furthermore there is another person I want to check out and I am hoping he is there when we get there."

"You know, when we went to the house where the dogs mauled that poor guy, I felt something was strange about the guy I interviewed. He kept saying the owner was out of the country however he would ever so often glance upstairs as if to see if someone was watching him," said Shane.

"Oh and you never saw anyone there?"

"No and I didn't have any real reason to go upstairs as I felt no-one actually saw the incident. They found the guy after the fact."

"One must wonder why the deceased was looking around the yard as all indications are he was Snake's main man."

Chapter 16

Matt had changed his outfit when James and Shane walked into Sarah's room and he was taken back, seeing them standing inside her room, "You guys are back already. Is there something going on officers?"

"Not at all Matt, we are trying to wrap up some things and we are hoping you can help us out, if you have the time," James said.

"Me? Not sure how I can help you but sure, what do you need to know?"

"Well, you see, we got a call shortly after Snake tried to see Sarah and there was some gun play in the parking lot. We were wondering if you knew anything about." James said.

"Aha, someone called you guys? Alright, I don't mind telling you what happened. I was on my way to get a change of clothes when someone drove a car directly at me and I tried to defend myself by firing at him, not sure if I hit him, but I shot out his driver's side window."

"May I ask if you have a permit for the weapon and if so, may we have a look at it?" James asked.

"Sure, here it is, and it is current," Matt said as he presented his card to James.

Returning the card, James asked, "Any description of the person and the car he was operating?"

"Nah, it was a big sedan with tinted windows. I believe I shot the driver."

"Ok Matt, here is my card, if you can think of anything else, feel free to give me a call."

Turning to Sarah, James asked, "How are you feeling?

A faint smile appeared but all she said was, "I am ok and the doctor said I would be released tomorrow."

Bidding her a good night, James and Shane stepped out of the room, spoke to the two officers stationed at the door and they were off.

"So Det. Williams, do you think Matt may have shot Snake and if so, where do you think he would go?"

"Shane, I think he did, he appears to be a person who knows how to handle a weapon. As to where Snake would go, it's anybody guess, but he certainly won't come back to this hospital. He might have a doctor who will patch him up, we will have to follow up on this and check around."

` ` `

Dropping Shane back at the station, he decided to call it a night and go on home; it had been a busy night for him in more ways than one.

Bev was restless in bed as she felt the need for James. Hearing the familiar sound of his footsteps coming in, she waited for him.

After a quick shower, he crawled into bed and snuggled up next to her and inhaled her scent. Turning over, she reached for his hands and placed them on her stomach and held them there for awhile and waited. He did not responded and in her frustration, she pushed away his hands and turned her back to him.

As he lay on his side feeling ashamed, he could hear her sobbing and coming to rest behind her, he tried to comfort her only for her to push him away again and walked to the bathroom. He knew he was in trouble but he didn't know exactly what to say to her; he could lie but she usually see through it. It might be best for him not to say anything at all, he thought and so he rolled over, covered himself and went to sleep. He knew the next day things were going to be a difficult and there was no escaping the questions.

Saturday morning he turned over and realized Bev never came back to the bed and she wasn't in the bathroom. Getting dressed, he cautiously walked to the kitchen where he saw her standing in front of the stove and he walked over to her.

Turning to face him, he walked away from his embrace. Hands on her hips, she glared at him, "Jimmy, exactly what's happening? You had no interest in me last night after all the talk about how much you appreciate me and happy in our marriage. Please tell me you are playing around. I need to know the truth."

"Honey, please don't think like, last night was a tough night for all of us at the station, I had to investigate two separate incidents which kept me busy and a bit stressed out. My feelings for you have not changed, you know that honey. Come here please, I am sorry, I tired last night but will make it up to you later."

"I am warning you, if I get the slightest idea you are screwing around, I am out of here with the kids. Remember two can play the game, other men are still interested in me if you are no longer interested."

Her last comment struck him like a sledgehammer; at no time did he even consider Bev playing the field and this frightened him.

"Come on my dear, you don't mean it, do you?"

"Well, you get involved with anyone else and wait and see. I don't want to but if you can't be true to me why should I keep myself for you."

Pulling her close, he embraced her as she reluctantly came into his arms. Holding her ever so tightly, he whispered, "I am yours and only yours."

` ` `

Candy was slowly getting up after a restful sleep; it had been a long time since she slept so soundly. Stretching out in her king-size bed, she rolled over and held on to the second pillow. Bringing it to her face; she smell James, and she loved the scent and wanted more.

Finally getting up, she strolled to her bathroom with a big grin, thinking she had never met a man before who made her feel so good. For the rest of the morning she strolled around naked; she didn't expect anyone to visit.

` ` `

It was late in the morning when Sarah was released; she only had a concussion and a broken scalp. Once fully examined, she was cleared to leave.

With Matt by her side, she slowly walked out of the hospital. While he wanted her to stay at his house, she wasn't yet ready. She still remembered why they broke up many years ago. Plus, she needed to sort out a number of things before she could even look at moving on, her children were still with Pearl and she wasn't sure they wanted to live with him.

As Sarah walked through the door, Pearl and the children rushed towards her, everyone chatting at the same time.

Slumping in the chair, she said, "Please guys, give me a minute and I will tell you all about it. It has been a difficult few hours."

Sharon was the first to speak, "Mom, where have you been since yesterday, you never called and what happened to your face?"

"My child, I became involved in an accident yesterday, and was taken to the hospital. I should have asked the nurses to call, but I wasn't thinking straight. Also I think Lucas tried to visit me there and he was involved in a shooting."

Pearl shouted, "Was he hurt?"

Glaring at her, Sarah said, "Why do you care if he was hurt?"

"Ah, I mean, I was hoping it was the end of him, you know, out of your life for good. What did you think I meant?"

"For a minute, I thought you were more concerned about his welfare than mine."

"Sarah, you know better than anyone else how I feel about him and often wish you would have left him a long time ago. No sister, I have no interest there, rest assured."

"Sorry for thinking like, my head is spinning right now, please forgive me. Kids, come over here and sit beside me for awhile."

Sharon and Sue sat on each side of her, "Girls, your father wants to make up for the time, he spent away from you."

"But mom, why would her? He hasn't been here for any of us," Sharon said.

"Maybe we could try again; he was my protector when Lucas tried to hurt me."

"We will see, it will take awhile as we hardly know him," replied Sharon.

The words cut deep in Matt's heart. He knew they were being truthful, "I can only try but I promise to be there for both of you and your mom. I will be on my way and hope to see you kids soon. "

"Ok girls, I need to speak with aunt Pearl, please give us a few minutes."

Once the children calmed down, they retreated to their room and Sarah and Pearl walked out to the pool.

Clutching her elbow, Sarah said, "I have told Jimmy all that I know about Lucas He has promised to help me with my case."

"Are you sure that's the only reason why you told him? Come on Sarah, it's me Pearl you are speaking to; I am not here to judge you. Tell me the real reason why you told him."

"I guess you know me too well Pearl, you know I care for him and yes I know he is married but I can't help myself. I figure if he were to arrest Lucas and put him away, I could get on with my life. You and I both know Lucas won't stop until he gets to me or worse, my children and I need him to be put away, one way or another."

"Ok, I can understand your feeling and fears but how does Matt come into the picture; you guys haven't spoken in years, what gives?" asked Pearl.

"Actually it was one of his vehicles I ran into yesterday and I guess the driver called him. He stayed with me for the entire evening and nigh; it made me felt safe lying there in the hospital. Jimmy has all the information on Lucas; I am not looking forward to spending time in jail.

"Sarah, let's not worry about it right now, you are here and you are ok."

` ` `

Looking at his tattered clothes beside him, Matt marveled how close he came to being run-over by Lucas. This had now become his war and he doesn't plan on backing down. He considered himself as a marksman and would have been surprised if none of the bullets had hit Lucas.

He would not allow Lucas to have a second chance at him; he would bring the war to his front door. He would take away his ability to make money, and his ability to have any control over his women.

Driving along Rich Street, he stopped at the traffic lights and looked around and smiled when he saw the Elves bar. "Interesting place" he thought as he pulled away.

Looking in his rearview mirror, he noticed a large truck right behind him and not thinking much about it, continued on his way. At the next stop light, he noticed the same truck still behind him but this time it did not appear to be slowing down. On his left and right, he realized there were pedestrians on both sides and with a calculated risk, spun his car around in the opposite direction and sped back up the road.

In the rearview mirror he watched as the truck ploughed into the car in front of it; pushing it into the middle of the intersection. He did not wait around to see the carnage but rather, he turned onto a cross street and went his way.

` ` `

For the better part of the day, James' head was in a fog; Bev words cut deep. He had been put on notice by her. For the first time in awhile, he was feeling like his world was slowly closing in on him.

He couldn't buy her any expensive gift as she would feel he was hiding his guilt. That was the last thing he could afford. Finally, he decided to leave early for work and complete a half shift, return home and try making it up to her; if only she would allow him.

He hadn't heard anything from Sarah or even Candy and he was hoping they would not call. He needed to stay focused and with the new information on Snake, it should not take him too long to find him.

He also knew the situation with the women could get out of hand and he needed to curtail it as soon as possible. Calling the station, he decided to take off half of his shift and spend the evening with Bev.

After contacting the station, he called Bev at her workplace. "Hi honey, guess what? I have taken the afternoon off and would like us to go out for dinner later."

"Why would you do that, are you trying to make up for what happened last night and what I said earlier today?"

"Yes and no, we need to spend a little more time by ourselves, away from the kids and a dinner date might be a good thing."

"I will have to think about it, what time were you thinking of going? I do have some errands to run after I leave here."

"Can't you put them off for another day? I am thinking of making a reservation for around six."

"No Jimmy, I can't put them off, remember I have a life too. I will try and meet you there if you want, give me the address."

"Ok, I guess we could meet there, here it is, and I love you."

"Me too but I have to go Jimmy, I will see you later."

The anguish in her voice told him, he had an uphill battle to overcome. He was also wondering what kind of errand she had as she usually tells him everything. Thinking of following her, he knew if she found out, it would be the end and he couldn't take such a chance.

During his shortened shift, he decided to visit the Elves bar, only this time, he planned to show his identification. As usual, there were drunks and homeless people walking aimlessly about.

Walking up to the front door and flashing his badge, he watched as the bouncers reluctantly stepped aside. Chili was still the main act however he wasn't interested in speaking with her; he wanted to speak with the other girls. However, no-one would provide any information and seeing he had no warrant, there was little he could do except promise to return.

From the corner of his eyes, he saw Chili lurking around yet staying a safe distance from him. With no luck, he walked out to run an errand before meeting Bev. Behind him, he saw the bouncers giving him the finger and he smiled and waved.

` ` `

Bev was still feeling upset with James, but smiled at the thought of them having a dinner date; it was something they had not done for awhile. Having no errands to run, she wanted him to try and figure out what she was doing. She felt it had worked by the way he sounded when she spoke with him. She was still in love with him and it scared her to think for a minute he might be fooling around.

It was time for James to meet her and he was running late. After picking up two of the children, he stopped by the flowers shop and got caught in the traffic. He eventually arrived at the restaurant a few minutes late and slowly walking through the door, saw Bev pacing the floor.

His eyes brightened when he saw her as he wasn't certain she would show up. Seeing him, Bev's frown changed to a slight smile and she walked towards him. He pulled the bunch of roses from behind his back and handed it to her as he kissed her on the cheeks.

"You are late," she said while gently sticking a finger in his side.

"Yes I am sorry, it took me longer than I had planned to get those for you," pointing at the roses.

"Well thank you, they are quite lovely."

As they each savored a sweet, succulent shrimp toss salad dish, they glanced lovingly at each other.

On the drive home, she held his right hand and gently squeezed it as soft music played in the background. They felt like young lovers and it brought back memories of when they were courting.

Later night as they slept in each other's arms, James' cell phone rang. Reaching for it while turning on the bedside light, he looked at incoming number; it was from his station. "It must be serious for you guys to be calling me at this hour, what's up?" he said.

"So sorry Det. Williams, we wanted to let you know there is a fire down on Rich Street tonight, the place is still burning."

"Which place is this, officer?

"It's the Elves Club, sir."

"Hell, are you serious, how did it happen?"

"We are not sure, but the Fire Marshall is down there now. I know you had some dealings there so we thought you would want to know. Anyways, sorry to have disturbed you, have a good night sir."

James sat up in the bed for a moment and said, "That's interesting information."

Bev sat up, and watching him she too wondered what had happened, "Is everything ok?"

"Yeah, just a night club on fire. We were watching the place for awhile."

After a few minutes they both settled back in the bed with her resting on his chest; listening to his heartbeat. While she didn't care to be woken up from a deep sleep, she felt ok to know it wasn't a call whereby he had to get up and leave her or from another of his street contacts.

` ` `

Matt stood a hundred yards off and watched as the patrons began to rush out of the Elves bar. The fire burnt slowly at first; giving the patrons a chance to get out before the building engulfed in flame. He chuckled as he saw several half naked women running out with their clothes in their hands and the bouncers were on their cell phones.

He knew it would be completely destroyed before the fire trucks would be able to get the fire under control. As the building continued to burn and set off several balls of fire, he walked away

Getting his car, he knew this was the beginning of his war on Lucas. In his mind thanked Sarah for letting him in on Lucas' business ventures. Now all he had to do was to destroy them one at a time.

The Fire Marshall was unable to enter the building due to extent of the fire and had to wait until it was brought under control. He noted there was a strange smell coming from the fire and while he could not determine what it might have been, he noted it certainly wasn't marijuana.

"How many people were in the building, do you have any idea?" the Marshall asked the bouncer.

"We are not certain as to the number, maybe 40 or so," he replied.

"Is everyone accounted for? What about the workers, how many are there?"

"Yes, all the workers got out safely. Can't say for sure about the others, we don't keep records of who comes in, sorry."

"For your sake, let's hope no one was left in there otherwise you will be held responsible for their death."

Sitting in the back of an ambulance, Chili, shivering as one of the medics brought her a blanket. She could not believe her luck, she   about to take a nap downstairs after completing her show. She had a room there and often times stayed there rather than go home. If it were a night when Lucas was there, he would have driven her home, but this wasn't one of those times.

She felt scared to think what might have happened if she had fallen asleep and the other girls were already gone. Borrowing a phone, she stepped out of the ambulance and walked some distance away from the group and dialed his number.

Chapter 17

It was 3:30AM when the phone rang and frightened Lucas. For a moment he could not locate his phone and eventually noticed the bright light flashing. Reaching across the bed, he grabbed it and said, "Who is this calling me at this ungodly hour? It better be for a good reason."

"Lucas, it's me, Chili, down by the bar."

"Is everything alright? You sound upset, what's happening?" he asked.

"Oh Lucas, there is a fire down here and I think the entire building has been destroyed. The Police and the Fire Marshal are all here. I don't know what happened, but luckily all the girls got out."

"Chili, are you telling me my building has been destroyed, what about the stuff downstairs, those are gone too?"

"I think so; you should see how the fire sent sparks high up in the sky. Nothing could survive in that heat. Will you be coming by?"

"All right Chili, if anyone ask you anything, don't say things except you are a dancer there, you don't know anything else. Make sure the other girls don't talk to anyone. I will be there as soon as I can. Where is your phone? This is not yours as your name did not show up on it."

Chili said, "I must have lost it when we were all running out of the bar, I have not been able to find it."

"That's not good Chili, you know if the Marshall finds it in the fire, he will be going through all the messages and I know you did not delete all of them as I told you to. Make sure you clear this number before you give back the phone and hope they don't find yours." Lucas said.

"Sorry Lucas, I wasn't expecting to run out of the bar because of a fire. I will see you when you get here. The same cop from last time; he came here early today asking the girls questions but they didn't say anything."

"Good, I will talk to them later."

Slamming down the phone, Lucas begun to punch the bed; he could not believe what he was hearing; his main bar burnt down. Most importantly, he had a shipment of cocaine in the basement he had planned to cut up and ship out to several of his contacts. He also knew the Fire Marshall and Police wouldn't stop until they found the cause of the fire and all the contents were in the building.

Feeling the noose tightening around his neck, a headache instantly came on. The Police was still on his case and his bosses in Central America were becoming impatient with him and his excuses.

In fact the bosses were thinking he was lying as no one person could have all those losses in such a short time. They would be sending one of their own to check on him. He had also made another enemy in Matt when he tried to run him down and didn't think there would be consequences.

Thinking hard, Lucas wondered who might have burnt down the bar if it wasn't an electrical fire. The only person he thought of was, Matt. "It had to be him; he knows I was the one who tried to run him down. I should have shot him the other day when he punched me. Now here I am with a broken arm and my bar burnt down, possibly by this idiot," he said to himself and began to curse once more.

With his limp arm, he struggled to get dress and slowly walked downstairs and out the door.

Arriving on the scene, Lucas stood from afar and viewed the destruction of his business; it was completely destroyed. The firemen were still pouring what appeared to be a powdery substance on the building. With his head covered by a large hat, he slowly edged closer to the spectators looking at the damage. Seeing the two bouncers and Chili standing aside from the main group, he walked over to them.

Chili was the first to see him, so she rushed into his arms but he held her off for a minute; he did not wish to draw any attention to himself.

"Not now Chili, if those guys see you talking to me they might want to ask me questions and right now I am not in the mood to be asked anything by them," Lucas said while looking in the direction of the Police.

"I understand, we were waiting for them as they said they wanted to ask us some questions," Chili replied.

"Now remember what I said to you on the phone, you know nothing and that goes for the girls and the guys too. I am going to try and see if I can hear what they are saying," he said as he began to walk away.

"Mr. Wise? Wait a minute, we were told you are the owner of this building. May we have a few words with you?"

As he turned around, sweat dripped down his arms even though the weather cool.

He asked, "Are you speaking to me, I am not the owner of building, sorry, you must be mistaken. I was passing by and saw all these trucks and people standing around."

Pointing to the crowd, the Marshal said, "Sorry Mr. Wise, these people told me you are the owner. I am Fire Marshall Dixon and I do need to speak with you, if not right now we can do it in my office or down at the Police station, your choice."

"Ok, ok, what questions do you need to ask me? Let's make it quick as I can't stay here too long."

"Let's go to my vehicle where we can talk without all the noise around us." And with that Marshall Dixon led the way to his car and opening the passenger door, invited him to take a seat.

Once inside, the door shut, Lucas jumped in fright at the sound of it locking. Sweating, he was vulnerable as he had never been in such a position before.

"Before we start, I must tell you I will be recording this conversation, do you understand?"

"Do I need to have a lawyer here before I answer your questions?" Lucas asked.

"No, as so far this does not appear to be a criminal act but we have yet to begin the investigation. As you can see, the fire is still smoldering so we will do it in a few hours. But I do have a question for you, why you were so against saying you own the property? Do all those ladies have their papers?

I am just asking," Marshall Dixon said.

"I try not to tell the world about my business as too many want hand-outs so I am always a bit cautious. To answer your other questions, yes, the all the women have their documents."

Marshall Dixon said, "Ok that's all for now but you do know if we find anything there we have to speak with you again."

"That will be fine. Can I go now? I don't like sitting here for others to see me; it does not help my image you know," Lucas said with a nervous grin. "You are free to go, we do know where to find you, have a good morning. Oh, one more question before you go. There is a foul smell coming from the building, any chance you would know what it might be?"

"Sorry, Marshal Dixon, I have not the foggiest idea what it could have been." Lucas said as his trembling hands opened the door.

Stepping out of the vehicle, his heart pounding hard, he held his chest as if to slow it down but it was no use; it kept beating fast. He didn't speak with anyone else and returned to his car.

Sitting for a few minutes, he thought of all the possibilities of how things might come crashing down on him. His remaining men were not of much use to him; all the good ones were dead and furthermore, he no longer knew who he could trust.

He was quickly given up by the patrons; the same people to whom he often provided free drinks and cocaine. He was now being questioned as to the status of the women dancing in his bar.

He felt the need to find Matt as soon as possible and eliminate him as he believed he had a hand in the destruction of his bar. But where would he find him? He knew little about this man and never even heard about him prior to seeing him with Sarah and Pearl.

"Sarah and Peal, now why didn't I think of them? Maybe they set him up to do this to me?" he wondered out loudly.

Having a general idea of where Pearl's house located and while he did not know where Sarah was staying, he decided he would try and find it. Rubbing his hands together, and with a sinister smile, he pulled away from the lot. He was going to be busy for the next little while and didn't care how long or what he had to do as long as he got his revenge.

` ` `

James rose quite early and walking into the kitchen, came behind Bev and placing his arms around her, kissed on the ears and said, "Good morning my love, had a good night?"

Turning to face him she smiled and said, "You know we both did, not only me. I hope you know you have a lot more to do to make up for the other night. Also, from now on, be open with me. You know if you don't tell me things I start thinking the worse."

"It's a promise, from now on, I will tell you my love," he replied.

"So what's this about the bar being burnt down last night?" she asked.

"Yes, that's what the officer said when he called. You know, I didn't even get his name but it does not matter, I am sure there will be a report on it when I get to the station. Anyway, we won't talk about work right now. I had a good time on our date last night; we should do it more often."

174

"Jimmy, I must say it was a nice idea even though I was upset with you, you certainly know how to get to me, thanks, and it was fun."

"The kids are getting bigger and can be left on their own for a few hours so yes we will try and do it more often. By the way, out of curiosity, what errands did you have yesterday?"

Laughing out, she said, "I never had any, I wanted to stress you out a bit and make you sweat and I know you did, I heard it in your voice."

"Yes, I must admit, I was taken back a little when you said it. Oh I almost forgot to tell you of the conversation Paul had with me the other day."

"Oh, what did he say?"

"He actually asked if I would consider taking the sergeant's exam and join him on the inside, funny eh?"

"And what was your answer?"

"Oh I told him I would consider it, maybe once I wrap up this case. We will see as this would be an opportunity for me to be able to spend more time with you and the kids."

"That's a good enough reason for sure. I hope you will give it some serious consideration though," she said.

` ` `

Sarah was restless; she had lost her car and would have to wait a week or two before she could get a replacement. She felt stranded and hated waiting on or depending on others to drive her around even though both Pearl and Matt offered. She wasn't in the habit of having to depend on anyone; not even Lucas.

While she lived with him, she was still an independent woman plus now she no longer in the home she had called her own for the past few years. She however also knew she could never return to be with him; there were too many signs he wanted to get rid of her too. She also coming to accept the fact it was the best thing she could have done was telling James about him.

She had to start looking out for her own welfare and only hoped James would do as he promised and speak with the crown on her behalf. Not waiting for the insurance company, she decided to go ahead to get herself another vehicle.

Calling Matt, she asked, "Do you have some time to take me downtown? I need to look at some vehicles."

"Sure, I would be happy to take you there. When you like to go?" Matt asked.

"How about later today, if you aren't too busy?"

"I'll see you shortly," Matt said.

` ` `

It was now time for James to report to the station and as he got dressed, Bev walked into the bedroom; handed him his phone and telling him; it had been ringing for some time now.

Looking at it, he saw it was Candy and his heart skipped a beat; waiting for Bev to ask. She simply gave it to him and walked back through the door. With a sigh of relief, he declined the call and slipped the phone in his pocket and joined her in the living room.

Turning to him, Bev asked, "Was that one of your contacts?"

Thinking quickly he responded, "She is a nurse we had to interview for a case and I had asked her to contact me if she recalled any new information. I had given her my card for her to call me or the station and I guess she decided to call me instead. I will follow up on this when I get in."

As he drove along the way, James marveled at the houses lined the road and the types of cars parked in their driveways. Some of them could be called mansions while others were the cookie-cutter types. Interestingly, in the driveways of the mansions, were the regular cars while on the other side, there were large SUVs' and exotic cars parked there. He figured how the rich remain rich; they don't spend their wealth on fancy cars but rather on their homes.

Looking at his phone, he decided to call Candy; he wanted to know what was so pressing she needed to call him so soon. They both had promised each other there would not be any pressure from either one of them. The phone rang four times before it was picked up.

On the other end, there was a long pause before the voice came and said, "Hello."

"I am sorry, I am looking for Ms. Buttons, is she there?" James asked.

"No, sorry, she is not available right now; may I ask who is calling?"

"Who am I speaking with?" asked James.

"This is her husband, now who am I talking to?"

Almost dropping the phone, James said, "This is Det. Williams."

"So Det. Williams, why were you calling Candy, what business do you have with my wife?"

"Ah, she is assisting us in an investigation so I am trying to follow up on it with her."

"But you are calling her private number, I would think you would be calling her at work, don't you think so, Det. Williams?"

"True, but she told me it would be alright to contact here."

"Would that also be the reason why you were at my house the other night?"

On hearing those words, James almost lost control of his vehicle and had to steady his nerves before he could answer. Candy told him she was single and here he was being confronted by this man who said he is her husband.

"Yes, it's true; I met her there due our schedules. Anyway, sorry to have bothered you have a good day," James said as he ended the call.

Mind racing, he wondered if Candy was ok and how much did her husband know about his visit; could he have been watching the house when he visited? All these questions and yet he had no answer so he decided one way or another, he was going to find out what happened. He would first go to the station then run over to the hospital and see if she there.

Candy was walking around her house when there was a knock on the door. Quickly donning a house-coat; she cautiously walked to the door and looked through the peep-hole. Standing there was, Michael. And he was irate.

Gasping in disbelief, she asked, "Why you are here and what do you want from me?"

"Candy, let me in, I'm not going to stay out here and talk to you through a closed door. I want to know what's going on, open the damn door," he said.

"Michael, we don't have anything to say to each other. You are no longer my husband and in case you forget, you don't live here anymore. I don't have to open this door to you anymore. Why don't you go away and find the woman you cheated on me with, you look like you are drunk, please go away."

As Michael continued to pound the door, he said, "Candy, I am warning you, if you don't open it, I will break down this door."

"Well, I guess you will have to break down the door because I'm not opening it," Candy said as hurried to the bedroom where she quickly got dressed.

While getting dressed, she called James and when she got no answer, she called the station.

From inside her bedroom, she heard an object pounding the door and she knew she had to get out otherwise he would do her harm. Grabbing her car keys, she rushed to the garage as front door gave way under his constant pounding.

By the time Michael was in the house, she was driving out of the garage and to her freedom. Looking for her telephone, she realized in her hurry, she had left it in her bedroom. "How could I have been so careless by leaving it back there?" she said while cursing herself.

Chapter 18

James arriving at his prescient and feeling stressed, he was afraid to think what might have happened to Candy. Sitting in his car, he surveyed the building and the surroundings, wondering with all his involvement, how he had lasted this long as a cop.

Walking to Sgt. Harris office, he knocked on the door, "Can I speak with you for a few minutes?" he asked.

"Of course, come in, I would be happy to chat for awhile. What's happening?"

"Paul, I need to tell you something but you must promise me it will stay between us, ok?"

"Of course Jim, you know me better than; we can talk openly with each other, what happening?"

"Well, a couple of nights ago, I met with a young woman, I called her house now and her husband answered the phone."

"What do you mean, you met her, am I correct in what I'm thinking?"

"Yes, you are. Now I am a bit concerned for her safety."

"You bastard, I never knew, but listen, it's safe with me, I have been down that road once. Why do you think I decided to take a desk job? The risk to my marriage was too great and Mary started asking too many questions," Paul chuckled.

"After all these years, I never knew and I did wonder why you gave up the street beat as I recall you use to enjoy it."

"So Jim, tell me about her, what is she like?"

"Well, she's a wonderful and kind woman. In addition to being a nurse, she is warm, pleasant, has a beautiful smile and a fantastic body. She told me she was unattached so it took me by surprise when a man answered her phone."

"What are you going to do?" Paul asked.

"I am going to skip out for a few minutes and drive to the hospital to see if she is there. If Bev calls, let her know I am on the road and will be back soon. I need to find out what happened to her."

"Ok, you know I have your back, take your time, we will be ok down here."

"Thanks Paul, it's good to know we can talk like this and it's appreciated. I will be back soon," and with that he walked out of the office.

"Det. Williams, there is a message from a Candy Button for you, here it is," said the young officer as he handed James the note.

Quickly looking it, he noted it only said someone had broken into her house and she was leaving for her safety.

Grabbing his gear, James raced out of the station; refusing the assistance offered by Shane. With his siren blaring, he whisked in and out of traffic and arrived at the hospital within five minutes.

Coming to an abrupt stop without properly parking, he rushed upstairs to the nurses' desk and there she stood. Fighting the temptation to pull her in his arms, he took a deep breath and slowly walked up to her and said, "Is everything ok with you? You got me scared."

At first, she did not see him coming but when she heard his voice, she became emotional and turning around, had tears in her eyes. She extended her hand to him as if to steady herself and he took it as a sign to lead her away from the desk, so they walked across the hall and sat down.

Wiping away the tears, her lips quivered as she tried to speak.

"You don't have to explain anything to me, I understand," as he put a finger over her lips.

He continued, "I was unable to call you back earlier and when I did, your husband spoke with me."

"But Jay, I do want to explain to you what happened. When I told you I was single, it's the truth, Michael, who you spoke to today, is actually my ex-husband and we have been divorced for the past six months. I divorced him because I caught him cheating and abusing alcohol," She got up and wring her hand, said, "Whenever he becomes drunk, he keeps trying to come back to me and making my life hell. This morning was no different except this time; he actually broke down my door and came inside. I tried to call you and ran out of the house."

Laughing out, he said, "There is some irony in all of this, don't you think? Here you and I got together and you know I am a married man."

Chuckling, Candy looked at him and holding his hands said, "I guess you are right but it's different; I guess now I have come to look at life in a different way."

James replied, "I understand where you are coming from. I want you to know Michael was picked up sometime after you called the station and you need to make a decision if you are going to have him charged or not."

"I don't wish to have him charged; I want him to pay for the damaged door and for him to leave me alone. I have moved on but he is not getting what he was hoping to get from the bimbo, it looks good on him," Candy said with a smile while wiping away her tears.

Looking at her, he said, "Ok, I will have my men withdraw the charge, and they will give him a warning and have him make plans to address the broken door. Right now, I must get back to the office as I do have some pressing business to finish."

"When will I see you next? I enjoyed the time we spent together and can't wait to be with you once more," she said.

"Candy, we will see how things go, right now I do have a lot on my plate and need to sort some things out. Why not let's play it by air right now and see how things go, remember, no pressure."

"All right, I will be fine, I won't pressure you but at the same time, I don't want to be a one-night stand, ok."

"No worries, you won't be, I need to work on the case has been under my skin for awhile. Right now, I must be going but I will call you later."

As he walked away, Candy and the other nurses kept watching him until he was out of sight.

Once he disappeared, all the ladies gave a collective sigh and crossed their hearts while looking at Candy. She knew what they were all thinking but chose to ignore it and walked away.

` ` `

Matt came to get Sarah and as he waited, he asked about the children however, they were nowhere to be seen; they had gone out with some friends for the afternoon.

Soon they were on their way and pulling out of the drive-way, he couldn't help but notice how well manicured the lawn. The shrubs were all neatly trimmed to the same height and the roses appeared to be bright in colour. He thought Pearl must be doing quite well for herself in order to have such a nice place.

As they drove along, Matt had many questions for Sarah including the relationship between James and her. "I notice how you look at policeman whenever he is around you. Did you guys have something going on? I hope you don't mind my asking as I was thinking, maybe you and I could try again," he said.

Staring at him, she said, "No, we don't have anything going on; I was told by Lucas to try and entrap him, that's all. As for you and me resuming our relationship, I have to think about, right now I can't begin to think about such things."

She wasn't prepared to speak about her feelings for James and while she enjoyed Matt's company, she wasn't ready for a relationship with him.

"You want to know what Lucas has done to me over the years. Let me tell you."

Rather than having her relive some traumatic experiences, Matt said, "No need to revisit such things right now, you will be fine. You are a strong woman and seeing the way you have protected our children, you will be ok."

Soon they arrived at the car dealership where Sarah spent a few hours looking at, and selecting a replacement vehicle. After a test drive an SUV, she selected a gun powder coloured vehicle and once the papers were signed, they left to celebrate. It would be ready for her within the next three business days.

Matt was a bit surprised when she took out her credit card and paid for the vehicle; he thought she was dependent on Lucas.

"Listen, Matt, I might be his woman but I do my own thing and don't depend on anybody. I make my own money and keep it for the children and myself. You thought I depended on him? No sir, not this woman, you must have forgotten, even back when you and I were together, you know I did my own thing."

"Yes, how could I forget Sarah, forgive me. Ok I guess lunch will be your treat today, right?"

"I don't have a problem paying. I am also grateful for your help with the accident and looking out for me back at the hospital, thank you."

"Don't mention it, the least I could do. I wish I had taken out Lucas though; at least we would know he could no longer be a threat. I am sure he is planning something right now," replied Matt.

` ` `

Lucas was prowling the streets when he saw Sharon and Sue with some friends and looking for a safe place to stop, he watched them from afar for several minutes. As they walked along the sidewalk, he pulled up next to them and called out to them.

"Sharon, Sue, how are you doing? I have not seen you girls for a few days, where are you staying now?"

The younger child, Sue blurted out, "With Pearl" before her older sister could stop her.

"So you and your mom are staying there, how is it there, don't you miss your home?"

Sharon said, "Lucas, our mom says we should not speak with you as you have been mean to her."

"Look kids, I am sorry, yes, your mom and I have had some differences but you know I would never hurt her or any of you. Why don't you let me take you to where you and your friends are going? Come on into the car and I will drive you there, it's kind of hot to be walking right now," he said while opening the back door.

When the children hesitated, he got out of the car and quickly pushed both girls into the back seat and shut the door.

Looking directly at their friends, he said, "Don't you dare say anything or I will come back for you both, go on and mind your own business."

With that, he sped off with both girls screaming in the backseat. While the friends began to cry, bystanders who witnessed it were soon on their phones calling the police. Eventually, the friends were able to stop crying long enough to call their parents and relayed what had happened.

"Please let us out. Lucas, why are you doing this? We don't want to go with you and where are you taking us?" asked Sharon while banging on the back of his seat.

He responded, "I am not going to hurt any of you, we are going home and you can call your mom to come and get you. I promise no harm will come to either of you, stop screaming and thumping the back of my seat."

"I need to go pee, if you don't stop, I am going to do it on your car seat," said Sue.

"Ok, ok, I will stop at the next fast-food place and we all will go in, but don't either of you try to escape, it wouldn't be nice. You hear me?" he said while reaching behind him to grab Sharon's arm and twist it.

"You are hurting me. Alright, we hear you, let her go to the rest-room, I won't try and run away; not without her," said Sharon.

Pulling into the parking lot, he parked far away from other vehicles and began to escort both children towards the store. He held onto an arm of each child and smiled whenever he passed other customers. As Sue was about to walk to the rest-room, Sharon shouted, "I too need to use the bathroom."

With all the attention on him, he smirked and released her arm and she walked with Sue into the restroom.

Inside the restroom, the children saw two older women washing their hands and touching one of them, Sharon said, "There's a man out there holding us against our will."

One of the ladies said, "Oh my God, that's awful, I am Tina and she is Marie, don't worry, we will help you. Can you describe this man for us?" said Tina, the elder of the two.

Sharon described Lucas and when Tina pushed open the door, she saw him pacing the floor. Once they identified him, Tina and Marie decided to create a diversion.

Pointing out their car to Sharon and Sue, Tina said, "I will open our car and when we give the signal, run to it and lie down on the back seat. Stay there until we get there, understand?"

Both girls looked at each other and nodded their understanding. Running out the doors, Tina and Marie shouted "Fire, fire."

Stumping towards Lucas, they knocked him over as others rushed outside. Sharon and Sue ran out the building through a side door and jumped in the back seat of the ladies' car and waited.

Lucas, getting up slowly after been trampled, brushed off his clothes and rushed to the ladies' restroom only to find there was no fire and it empty. Exiting, he saw only the servers standing behind the counter.

Pushing open the entrance door with all his might, the door came back and hit him in the face. Wiping his busted nose, he cursed and ran to his car before driving out of the lot.

"Ok girls, he is gone, you can straighten up now. Why was he holding you against your will?" asked Marie.

Sharon said, "He and our mom broke up and we had to move. Now he doesn't know where we are staying and he was trying to get back at mom."

"That's just awful, my God. We must call the Police," Marie said.

"No, please, can you take us to this address, our mom must be worried about us and we don't have a phone to call her. By the way, I am Sharon and this is my sister Sue."

"Hi Sharon and Sue, you are safe now, we will take you home as it's along our way home. Here is a phone, call your mom."

` ` `

James heard about the kidnapping of two young girls and it bothered him. It was his distaste for men who abused young girls which led him on this chase for Snake.

Now, here was another man doing the same thing and he was upset. He had made it his life's job to hunt down such evil men and this would not be any different. Gathering as much information as he could, he called Shane, "We need to check the witnesses' statements and catch this SOB. We can't afford to have another person like that harming our children."

Half an hour later and after speaking with six witnesses, it was clear to James it was a kidnapping. All witnesses basically provided the same description of the offender and the vehicle.

Looking at each other, James and Shane thought they knew exactly who they were looking for and to confirm the information, they ran the license plate number.

Viewing the files in front of them, both men pumped their fists as James said, "We have him now, no longer are we going to wait for him to come to us, we are going after him today as those girls might be sold by tomorrow. The parents must be going out of their minds and it's my intention to bring those children back to them."

` ` `

Sarah was finishing her meal when a friend called her, "Sarah, where are you, my daughter called me to say someone kidnapped Sharon and Sue. He just pulled up near the children and grabbed them."

Screaming, Sarah began to bawl, "My babies, he took my babies, the son of a bitch grabbed Sharon and Sue. Ok, I got to go home, I will talk to you later, bye."

Looking at Matt as the tears flowed down her cheeks, her lips trembled, "Lucas has our babies, and I am going to kill him. I knew he would do something like this, since he couldn't get to me, he is using our children. Matt, I have to go home, let's go."

"Sarah, don't go and do anything that will make your situation any worse, I will take care of it, I will take you home as I am sure he will call you and use them as barter. Please don't think the worse right now, I will deal with him, take a few deep breaths, it will be over soon," Matt said.

Within a few minutes they were on their way with Matt travelling as fast as the traffic would allow him.

While pulling at her hair, Sarah's phone vibrated as a call came though and looking at it, she could not identify number and she cautiously answered, "Hello?"

"Mom, it's us Sharon and Sue."

Sarah said, "Oh my god, where are you, are you safe?"

"Yes mom, we were ok, we are on our way home to Pearl, these two nice ladies are taking us there and we will be there soon. We will tell you all about when we get home, mom, we love you."

"I love you both," she replied.

Looking at Matt, Sarah said, "They are safe and are on their way home right now with some ladies. I don't know what happened but thank God they are ok."

"Well Sarah, I told you not to think the worse, it will work out but we will still get Lucas."

Soon Matt and Sarah pulled into the driveway as Tina and the girls got there and they watched as the children dashed out of the car towards the house.

Sarah jumped out of the car before it came to a halt, and called out to her children who turned around and began running towards her.

Kneeling to hug them both, she began to kiss each and cry as Tina and Marie came to her side, "I don't know how to thank you ladies. You have saved my girls. Please come inside for a moment. I need to know what happened."

Once safely behind the closed doors, the children began to relay the events and how the ladies saved them from Lucas.

Matt and all the ladies could not believe what they were hearing; it sounded as if it was straight out of a movie. All they could do was to look at each other.

Sarah said, "Kids, I am so proud of you."

Looking at the ladies, she said, "Thank you so much for your kindness. I don't know what would have happened if you weren't there."

Soon Tina and Marie were on their way and feeling elated knowing they had helped to save the children.

While looking in a distant place, Sarah picked up her cell phone and dialed James' number but he did not pick up; she would not stop calling until he answered.

` ` `

James phone rang and looking at it, he noted it was from Sarah and so he disconnected the call until it rang once more. Picking it, he answered angrily, "Why are you calling me Sarah? I have told you... what? Those were your children? I am actually on the case right now, and we now know who it. I never guessed they were your children. Have you heard anything from them or Snake?"

"Oh James, some ladies helped them to escape and they are now here with me," Sarah replied.

"Ok, that's good news, what's your address? I will need to speak with them as soon as possible."

"Here is the address and to let you, Matt is here with me too."

"Why are you telling me this? I don't have a problem with him being around you; actually I think it might be a good thing. A couple of us will be there soon and don't open the door for anyone until we get there."

Lucas was feeling defeated in many ways; he could not even carry out a simple kidnapping of two young children. Looking in the mirror, he could not say who he had become; he had become a fragment of the man he once was.

He had one last opportunity to redeem himself and rebuild his empire by getting rid of the Policeman, Sarah and her boyfriend. Now he knew Sarah was staying with Pearl. No longer would he wait, he would make his move later in the night.

Walking into his closet, he opened a false wall and looked inside; there he examined his arsenal of weapons. Selecting selected four hand guns, he threw them on the bed.

For the next few hours while sitting in his living room, he loaded and unloaded each gun a number of times as he drank straight from a bottle of whiskey by his side. He looked around at all the things he once thought meant a whole lot to him and couldn't find any satisfaction in any of them.

They meant nothing to him as the house was empty; no children playing in their rooms and no Sarah to talk with. Even when they were involved in a heated argument, it was better than the silence he now faced. He always hated the silence as it caused him to think of too many bad things he had done in the past.

Chapter 19

It was just past 7PM when James and Shane pulled into Pearl's driveway. After looking around the property, they decided to park on the road instead so their escape route would not to be blocked. Hurrying towards the house, their heels bounced against the concrete walkway. The house towered over the trees, stealing the sunlight from the flower beds.

Climbing the steps, both men remained silent with their own thoughts and soon James knocked on the door and waited.

"Who is it?" asked the voice on the other side of the door.

"It's Det. Williams and Const. White, we are here to speak with Sarah, may we come in?"

"Just a minute officer," said the female.

Heavy footsteps echoed against the tile flooring as they approached the door. Slightly opening it, the woman looked through the half-cracked door. James and Shane both had their identifications out to show her as she opened the door completely.

Walking in, they saw a large well appointed living room off the foyer and sitting around an enormous table were Matt, Sarah and her two children.

"I'm Pearl, we met briefly the other day, welcome to my home, you know

Sarah and I think Matt, those are Sarah's children. Please have a seat; may I get you both something to drink, officers?"

"Yes, I do recall, thanks Pearl but no, we are fine. It's good to see you again Matt, Sarah, how are you feeling?" James asked.

"I am doing ok James but I am concerned for my children's safety."

Sitting down at the table, James said, "Sarah, seeing your kids are under age, we need your permission to speak with them."

"Yes, of course, you have our permission," said Sarah.

"Our, did you say our as in our children?" James asked.

"Yes, Jimmy, they are Matt and my children; we never advertised it. Everyone at this table knows so, yes, they are our children," Sarah said.

"Ok, we do need to speak individually with them. Const. White here will speak with the younger child while I speak with the older one. You said her name is Sharon, right?'

"Yes, I'm Sharon," she said with a smile.

Walking into a smaller room, James followed Sharon and sat opposite to her. For the next half an hour, she repeated what she told her mother.

James thought she appeared quite confident and brave and he too told her he was proud of her.

After he completed his interview, they both sat there for a few minutes before she said, "May I ask you a question officer?"

"Sure Sharon and please, call me James. What is it you would like to know?"

"Are you going to catch Lucas and if you do, what is going to happen to him afterwards? I know he got my mom to be involved in some bad things but I need to tell you, she is not a bad person."

"Well, Sharon, I can promise you I intend to find him and have him locked up as soon as possible. I don't want you and your sister to be afraid anymore. I am sure your mom is a good person, too bad she got mixed up with him."

"Do you sometime go by the name Jimmy, I often hear mom talking about a Jimmy and I wondered if you are the person she called about this," she said.

Smiling, he looked at her and said, "Yes, I am the person with whom she has spoken."

"Do you like her? I know she doesn't care much for our father out there; he never played any role in our lives. He is now coming around but I can see how she looks at you," she said while pointing to Matt.

"It's ok, you don't have to answer, I think I know the answer already, I know she likes you but for whatever reason, it didn't work out," Sharon said.

"Well, for a young lady, you certainly understand a lot, maybe one day if given the chance. I will tell you all about it but right now, I must speak with Const. White and see how best to get Lucas so he does not try to hurt you both and your mom. Thank you for speaking with me."

Walking back into the main room, James and Sharon sat down and waited for Shane and Sue to come back into the room. They too would soon join the group within a few minutes and sat at the table, planning their next move.

While everyone was busy chatting, James heard a rustling outside a window, "Turn off the lights and stay low. Shane and I will check this out."

"Do you guys need my help?" Matt asked.

"No, stay here with the women," James replied.

` ` `

Walking around to the side of the house, Lucas looked through the window and was taken back when he saw all the people sitting there. He had expected to see the girls, their mother, her friend and maybe the guy, Matt but now there were two other people.

Trying to get a better look inside, he stepped on some broken tree branches and cursed himself for not checking where he was walking.

Staggering on his feet, he thought; maybe he should not have consumed so much alcohol and cocaine before leaving his house. It was too late to do anything about it now. He was there for one purpose and   that was to kill Sarah and Matt if it was him in there with them.

He kept trying to convince himself as much as had tried to kidnap the girls, he wasn't the type to hurt them and wouldn't start now.

"My only intention was to use them as pawns in my attempt to get to their mother," he said.

Deep down, he knew that was not true. Looking back through the window, he could no longer see inside the house. The lights were off and it was pitch black. So here he was on the outside in total darkness except for the moon light casting his shadow on the wall. With his gun in front of him, he crept slowly towards the back of the house.

` ` `

James quickly slipped through the back door while Shane remained on the inside and with both their guns drawn; they waited for Snake to make his move. After waiting for a minute or two, James began to move towards the noise; he saw the shadow cast by the moon and it was coming towards him.

Seeing a hand holding a gun sticking out around the corner, he fired at it. The screams echoed in the quiet night and the weapon fell as footsteps hastily retreated. Picking up the gun, James called Shane, "Come on out, Shane, we have him on the run. This time we won't let him get away."

Rushing to their car, they began chasing the assailant. They soon caught up with the car as it drove recklessly down the road; at times riding the median. James called in the chase but as he already knew who the car belonged to and it made him even more determined to stop Snake at any cost.

Coming alongside the car, James shouted, "Pull over now. You won't get away Snake."

With a blank stare Snake pulled his car alongside James and slammed into the side, only to speed away.

James having reached a boiling point pulled back behind the car and pitted him and watched the car going into a tailspin. When it finally stopped, it was partially in a ditch and Snake jumped out, limping and firing his weapon.

James and Shane took cover at the side of their car as James shouted at him, "Snake, this is the Police, put down your gun and put your hands above your head."

Snake responded by firing at them. With Shane at the rear and James near the front of the car, both men fired their weapons in unison.

Blood began to seep from Snake's wounds as he felt numbness in his chest. Staring at his wounds, he couldn't believe he had been shot and dying. Taking deep breaths, he tried to raise his gun but he was becoming weaker by the seconds. Eventually, he fell onto his knees and stayed there.

James snatched the gun from Snake's dying hands as well the one used by Shane and called in the shooting. Searching the car, he found two other hand guns lying on the front passenger's seat; fully loaded. Both men remained at the scene until the coroner and other Police officers arrived and took over the investigation.

Returning to Pearl's residence, James informed them, "Snake was killed in the shoot-out."

Sarah and Pearl both clasped their hands over their mouths; they had no idea it was him outside the house. Looking at each other, they both knew without saying a word, had he gotten into the house, they would all have be dead.

The children began to cry and the ladies held them close to try and comfort them. While Lucas had tried to kidnap them, they also lived with him for a few years and shared some kind of relationship.

A week later, the Police completed their investigation and the guns were returned to James and Shane. The coroner confirmed what James already knew; Snake was high on drugs and alcohol and would most likely have killed everyone in the house, if he had gotten the chance.

`` ` ` ` ``

The Police and the Court began the process of seizing all of his assets including his motor vehicles and known properties except one. Along the way, Chili was picked up for her part in procuring under-age girls for, among other things, prostitution and dancing in the Elves bar.

In their search, the Police also found information on Snake's South American contacts and these they passed onto the relevant authorities.

The local newspaper ran a story on the take-down while mentioning James and Shane as the main force behind it. As usual, James did not wish to take all the credit so he made sure to include all members at his station including Sgt. Harris. Both he and Shane would be given commendations for their bra.

With Snake now dead and the case partially closed, James decided it was time for him to take a well deserved vacation; he would take off a couple of weeks to catch up with his family and not to think about the job. Walking out of the station with Shane, he enquired as to the status of his friendship with Greta.

Grinning widely, Shane said, "We are spending a lot of time together at her apartment. I'm not yet ready to live there full-time but we are getting to know each other

"I don't blame you at all, make sure she is the one because others will cross your path and the temptation can be strong, and take it from me son, there will be many."

"Thanks Det., I will remember, especially coming from you," Shane said while laughing.

"Now why would you say that, are you saying I am guilty of such thing? Youngman if you only knew but I won't tell. I almost forget to say, congratulations on your promotion to become a first class constable, good for you."

"Thanks, it's all because of your assistance and believing in me."

"Well son, take care of yourself until I return and stay out of trouble," James said.

` ` `

Sarah and her children were still in shock days after the shooting and while it wasn't something new to her; the children were never exposed to such violence before. They were having nightmares and were afraid to sleep in their individual rooms; mother and daughters would eventually sleep in the same room.

She was relieved knowing that Lucas was killed. It was the only way she would have been able to escape him. Now that he was gone, his men no longer had a leader and would possible disband. All she had to worry about now was to get through the pending court case and she hoped for the best.

Walking out to the pool side, Pearl noticed Sarah sitting there and joined her with a drink for each of them and said, "Sarah, what are you going to do, now that Lucas is dead?"

"Pearl, one of the best things I ever did was to have my name listed as part owner on the house when we lived with him. It took some fighting with him but it was one of my conditions for living with him. When things settle down, we will move back into it."

"Good for you, Sarah, I always thought you were a smart woman. Of course, you can stay here even though I wonder if I should sell it. It might be time for me to move on. I need to do something worthwhile with my life."

Reaching for her drink, Sarah said, "Thank you Pearl, you have been the one person who I could count on; no matter what is going on in your life or mine, you have always been there for me. No need to sell your beautiful home. Well, let's not think about it right now. Let's enjoy this time while we can."

` ` `

Bev heard about the shooting before James told her and she was relieved, he had finally dealt with Snake. Now she felt less stressed out but she did not plan to share her feelings with him yet; he still had some making up to do.

James strolled into the kitchen and stood beside her; both looking out the window at the two younger kids playing in the yard.

Hugging her tightly, he said, "We do have some wonderful kids, thank you for being a great mother and wife."

"Well thank you Jimmy, that's a nice thing to say. Yes we do make great kids, don't we?"

"We sure do. You know something? I have been giving some serious thoughts about taking the sergeant's exam. I am getting a bit tired of the streets and our kids are growing fast and I have missed a lot already."

Smiling widely, she turned to him, "Oh that would make me happy, it would mean less worrying about you and these late nights. I am sure Paul will help you in any way he can."

"Oh, I am sure he would, but I want to do this on my own. If I am going to do this, it's important I do it myself. I will go down to the station in a day or so and fill out the application. I also need to go over to the Courthouse to wrap up a case involving Snake's former partner."

"Would you like me to go with you? I could also see Paul as we haven't been around their home for a while now and we can go over to the Courthouse."

"That's ok if you wish but I am not sure you would enjoy going to the courthouse with me as they will have to scan you and you know how much you hate those scanners."

"True, but I don't mind this time, we can go for lunch afterwards."

"It's settled, we will do."

` ` `

As the court date drew closer, Sarah began having panic attacks. She hoped James had kept his word about helping her. She thought about calling him but felt she may push him away. Even though he had told her the affair was over, she still had hopes.

True to his words, James spoke with the crown attorney about her involvement with Lucas and his gang. An agreement was made which benefitted her.

James planned to return on the day of the trial and hopefully closed the file once and for all.

` ` `

Candy also heard the news about the killing. She had not heard from James for some time and wondered if he had forgotten her.

Deciding to give him a call, she dialed his number but the call disconnected before it went to the voice mail. On her second attempt, the call went to the voicemail and she left a message for him saying, "Jimmy, I hope you are ok, looking forward to seeing you soon. Do give me a call when you can."

James and Bev were on their way when his phone rang and seeing the caller id, he disconnected the call but not b3fore Bev saw it.

"Who was that and why didn't you answer the call?"

"The hospital was calling and I can deal with it later or have one of the guys at the station deal with it since I am on vacation."

"Jimmy, I know it's not from the hospital, it's same individual, who called you before. I do notice things. Do we need to have a conversation about all these calls? Right now, deal with whatever you got going on, I understand you had to do things to get this case resolved but it can't go on."

"There is nothing happening that you should be worried about, my love, I promise you, and it's all part of the job. Once this court case is done, all this will be behind us."

```
` ` `
```

At the station, James spoke in private with Paul, "I am thing about taking the exam."

"That's great news Jim but what made you decided to do it? You have been avoiding it for so many years. Have you spoken with Bev about your decision?"

"Yes, as I told you before, we have talked about it and you know she has been bugging me for ages to leave the street beat. I am not getting any younger as you often reminded me and I am not sure I want to spend the rest of my days chasing these idiots."

"Good for you, I look forward to you joining me soon, here are the papers to be filled out

"While we are here, I need to make a call for your ears only; I can't have Bev hear this right now."

"Sure, do you want me to leave while you make the call?"

"No, it would be suspicious; you can hear what I have to say."

"Hello Candy, sorry I missed your call, what's happening?"

"Hi Jay, I called because I wanted to know when you want to catch up, you know."

"Sorry, I won't be able to do it now; I am on vacation for a little while and plan to be away with the family."

"Ok, well, when you get back, why don't you give me a shout? I will be waiting but not too long, I need to see you."

"We will have to see how it goes."

"It sounds as if you are not interested in being with me. Am I correct in thinking that way?"

"Ah, Candy, it's not that I am no longer interested in you but you know I do have my commitments and those come first. Listen, I have got to go as Bev and I are out right now, I will call you when I can."

"Alright but remember what I told you, I don't want to be seen as a one night stand, I like you and thought you liked me too."

Rolling his eyes, he looks at Paul while speaking, "I have got to go, and we will talk soon."

"That's a live one there Jim, be careful she does not cause you and Bev any headache."

"I am hoping the same and I know I will have to deal with it soon. Right now we are going over the Courthouse to wrap up something."

` ` `

James soon stepped through the courtroom great big doors and saw Sarah in the prisoner's box. On seeing him, she smiled but it quickly turned to a frown when she looked at the woman beside him. Seeing Bev for the first time, she actually felt jealous of her.

After listening to the lawyers making their submission, clearing his throat, the judge said, "Ms. Brown, having pled guilty and assisted the Police in their investigation, I hereby sentence you to two years less a day. You will then be placed on three years' probation."

Hearing the sentence, she collapsed onto the floor. When she came around, tears flowed like a stream down her cheeks.

While being taken back to her sell, she called out, "Johnny, help me please."

Hissing, Bev asked, "Jimmy, why is she crying for you?"

"She was my first contact to find Snake and we had built up a relationship. She asked that I speak with the crown which I did so that's why her sentence is less than it should."

"Well, now the case is over, let's hope this will be the last time all these people will be calling you. I don't want to keep asking you about all these calls. I understand you had to do things to complete this case but no more."

Holding her hand, he looked her in the eyes and said, "No, there shouldn't be any further contact from any of them." In his mind, he prayed those words wouldn't prove to be his downfall.

The End

Vassell Ramsay

www.ingramcontent.com/pod-product-compliance
Lightning Source LLC
Chambersburg PA
CBHW030315180626
46810CB00003B/1090

PRAISE FOR *I, SEAN/A*

"Each of us is born with the God-given expectation of respect, dignity, and opportunity. And all of us know that along the path of life there will be challenges. Sean/a has encountered the unique challenges that come with being born intersex. What she shows in life and in these pages is a head held high with the warm smile of confidence, determination, and joy."
—Lisa Middleton, Former Mayor, City of Palm Springs

"In this profound and uplifting true story, Sean/a's extraordinary journey from homelessness to a life of purpose and fulfillment exemplifies the boundless potential of resilience and courage. With the compassionate guidance of a devoted benefactor, Sean/a's transformation becomes a testament to the life-changing power of empathy, perseverance, and an unshakable belief in what is possible. A must-read for anyone seeking proof that kindness and determination can illuminate even the darkest paths."
—Arielle Ford & Brian Hilliard, fans of Sean/a's

"This inspirational story of kindness, trust, and immense generosity illustrates that consistent and dignified resources truly make a difference and can be lifesaving. *I, Sean/a* motivates one to pay it forward."
—Claudia G. Grasso, Executive Director, One Safe Place
The San Diego County Family Justice Center

"If you could read only one book that embodies the incredible power of the human spirit's resilience, courage, and HOPE even in the darkest moments, THIS IS THE BOOK YOU'VE BEEN WAITING FOR. With grit, compassion, and vulnerability, Dr. Harrison and Sean/a take you through some of life's truly unimaginable challenges that ultimately lead to deep, lasting transformation. What a gift and a treasure this book is—reminding all of us that the pain and struggles that crack our souls wide open are where the brightest light seeps in to wake us up to the Goodness of who we really are."

—Renee Kohn, MA, SEP, Somatic Practitioner, Television Host

"A compelling inside look at life on the streets for one young, talented American who had a few too many bad breaks, and a community that came together to restore their dignity by offering a path out of homelessness. Dr. Harrison weaves together determination, faith and the generosity of community members to be a safety net to one in need. The result serves as an inspiration for each of us to continue our efforts to end homelessness for the hundreds of thousands of individuals that live without adequate shelter due primarily to the critical housing shortage in America."

—Steve Carlson, PsyD, University of Minnesota

"This compelling story of Sean/a's journey from adversity to transformation is a deeply inspiring testament to the resilience of the human spirit. From heart-wrenching to heart-warming, the depths of Dr. Harrison's unwavering support and guidance shine as a beacon of hope, demonstrating the life-changing impact of compassion, care and connection."

—Johnny Blackburn, Founder and Director of Mystics